To Be Wicked With You

League of Unweddable Gentlemen, Book 4

TAMARA

COPYRIGHT

CHAPTER 1

1827, Marlborough, Wiltshire

inley Stone, Duke of Carlisle, stared blankly at his solicitor. He would not believe what he'd been told. His father would not control his life, even after death. His decree would not be borne.

"Excuse me, Smithers, but can you repeat what you just said? I'm sure I did not hear correctly."

His solicitor cleared his throat, lifting the parchment yet again. "You have been the duke for one year, may your father rest in peace. However, I am now at liberty to tell you that your father put in a stipulation to his will. If you do not marry within one year of his death, you have sixty days from the anniversary of his death to do so. If you fail this stipulation, the bulk of your fortune, the money, and any assets not entailed, will revert to your cousin, Andrew Stone of Kent."

Finn leaned back in his chair, running a hand through his hair. His mind balked at the idea of marrying. Not to mention what men were supposed to do with the opposite sex. The idea of being forced into that occupation both terrified and excited him. It terrified him more.

"So I would keep Carlisle Hall in Wiltshire, but will have no money to keep the estate running other than the income it produces, which we all know is not enough."

"That's right, Your Grace. As the owner of several profitable estates, to lose those to your cousin would financially impact you severely. And have devastating consequences for those who rely on your estates for their livelihood. I would suggest you marry posthaste, retain your assets, and secure your future as soon as possible."

A wife? His stomach clenched, and he turned to stare out the window. He couldn't lose his home, the only place he'd ever loved. God knows his wicked father had been too busy carousing London to care about his family at home.

His mother had passed when he was eight, and his father had rarely bothered with him. Finn had promised to be a better person than that. Someone his servants and friends would respect, a landlord who was reliable and not flippant.

"Well then, I suppose I have to return to London and find a bride."

His solicitor cleared his throat, and Finn looked up, meeting his gaze. "Is there something else that I should be aware of, Smithers?"

"Your father has decreed that you are to find a wife here in Wiltshire. Someone local to Marlborough is preferable. He's decreed you marry a woman from your home county as he thought it would be better for the staff if they have a mistress who is familiar with the area and the local peoples."

Finn stared blankly at his solicitor. Was his father mad? Quite possibly, before his death and his wayward ways in

London. Finn certainly had thought his sire had lost his mind. But a wife from Woodstock? There were only two noble families living close by, if he could call them that at all.

One family had several daughters, all of them under the age of ten. They would never do. The second family, The Miltons… Finn tried to remember the dynamics of the family. The father was a gentleman, living off the income from his small estate. He doubted there was any dowry for any of the girls. They did, however, have a son, although he was still in short coats.

"In effect my father is stating I need to marry one of the Milton girls, whom if I remember the number correctly is a total of two."

Smithers nodded, coming to sit in the chair before his desk, rustling through the paperwork in his leather satchel. "That's right, Your Grace. The eldest Miss Milton is beyond marriage, but her younger sister, Lucy, is not."

"Who is the oldest Miss Milton again?" Finn asked, a face echoing through his mind from last season when he was in town.

"Ah," Smithers said, searching further through the paperwork. "Miss Evie Milton. I believe she is friends with the Duchess of Whitstone and her social sphere."

A vision of a dark-haired beauty that was well on her way to being on the shelf entered his mind. He'd danced with her if he recalled, their conversation somewhat awkward since she'd been less than engaged to speak. Surprising really, considering her and her friends were some of the most opinionated women in the *ton*.

"Does not Miss Milton live in London in Marchioness Ryley's townhouse?" He frowned, certain he'd heard that after the marquess's marriage, the marchioness had allowed her friends to remain in her London townhouse. Miss Milton being one of them.

"That is correct, Your Grace."

"Hmm." Finn leaned back in his chair, wondering what the younger Lucy Milton looked like. If she were as striking as her sister, she would do very well indeed. She was young still, from a respectable family, and the local area. All requirements that would satisfy his late father's will.

"Do you expect Mr. Milton has any dowry for his daughters?" Not that it mattered, he was beyond wealthy and could afford to have a wife who came with very little or nothing at all. Even so, providing for female children on the off chance that you do not produce an heir told Finn a lot of a man's character. Whether they were loving, forward-thinking, and honorable. All the characteristics his father was lacking.

"Two hundred pounds per annum. The elder Miss Milton came into her stipend when she turned twenty-five. Of course, they assumed she would be married by then, and well, that did not occur. The younger Miss Lucy is two and twenty years of age."

"Very good. Well then," Finn said, standing and bringing this meeting to an end. "Tomorrow I'll commence my courting of Miss Lucy Milton and have it all settled by month's end. I will call for you when everything is in place."

Smithers bowed. "Very good, Your Grace. I wish you well in your endeavors and look forward to hearing the happy news."

"Yes, well..." Finn said, sitting back down and watching his solicitor stride from the room. Happy news may be too much of an exaggeration. More like resigned would fit in this context.

Finn pulled a piece of parchment toward him, picking up his quill and scrawling a letter for Mr. Milton to expect him tomorrow at eleven. He would not tell the gentleman as to why, merely let them believe it was a natural attraction and courtship that will bring him to offer for Miss Lucy. That would be best.

One thing he did comprehend was that no bride wanted to hear her betrothed only asked out of necessity. Or, in this case, the pain of disinheritance.

CHAPTER 2

Three weeks later, Marlborough Wiltshire

 $\mathcal{T}$ he carriage turned into the short drive of her family's home on the outskirts of Marlborough, her sister's hastily written letter the week before burning a hole in her gown. It was pure luck that it had taken her a week to organize travel to Wiltshire from London, for she needed a week to prepare herself for the realization that her younger sister was getting married.

The last time she had heard from Lucy, she hadn't mentioned a word about His Grace, so now to be engaged to him was out of nowhere. Her sister, although high-spirited, was not a silly woman prone to hasty decisions. To be marrying the wicked rakehell, Duke of Carlisle had made her think her sedate, intelligent sister had lost her mind. She would speak to her parents when she arrived, ensure for herself that they too had not lost their minds regarding their daughter marrying a duke.

No doubt, they were overcome with joy at the thought of Lucy marrying into such a lofty title. The duke was their closest neighbor, but never before had he ever shown an interest in the family. Evie glanced out at the passing oak trees that lined the driveway. She'd danced with him in London, had been a little distracted at the time with her friend's tribulations that evening, but she could still remember his scent. Sandalwood and spice. His hands had been large and strong against the small of her back. She'd had to look up to meet his gaze, and the memory even now made her shiver. One glance from the wicked Duke of Carlisle and one's knees went a little weak.

So handsome with his cutting jaw and perfect, straight nose. His smile was deadly, and his intense, heated stare worse. Not that she had been on the receiving end of such a look, oh no, he'd shown little interest in her. In fact, he'd seemed bored and uninterested in her attempt at small talk to pass the minutes of the dance, Evie had eventually pretended to be having a lovely time in his arms while counting down the minutes to the end of the dance. She had watched him at times in the *ton* and envied the women who did capture his attention. How lucky they would be to have such a rogue caught by their loveliness.

That her sister had captured his heart left her at odds. She was happy for her, of course, but a part of her also wished she'd found such a man herself. To marry, to love and be loved in return. Evie sighed, slumping back into the velvet squabs. She supposed it would not happen now. Not at her age, but at least she could content herself with being an aunt someday. Spoil her nieces and nephews to her heart's content.

Her sister deserved all happiness bestowed on her. She was the sweetest person who Evie knew, other than her favorite friends in London.

The carriage rocked to a halt before her family's

Georgian manor house. Evie stared up at the golden stone home that shone like a beacon in the afternoon sun. The many windows glistening and welcoming her home.

A footman opened the door, and she stepped down, taking his hand for assistance. "Thank you," she said, starting for the house. A horse stood tied to one of the hitching posts near the front of the residence, and a dreadful thought entered Evie's mind.

Please don't be the duke's beast. She needed to speak to her parents and talk to her sister alone. Ensure this was a welcome marriage. Not merely because a duke offered for a woman who only lived close by. Their lack of a substantial dowry at least told Evie that the union was based on affection.

Evie pulled off her gloves as she strode toward the entrance, glancing up as the door opened and Lucy stood before her, taller than she remembered, but just as beautiful with her golden locks and lithe figure. Evie smiled. "Lucy," she said, laughing as her sister all but ran toward her and threw her arms about her back. "You've grown!" she said, her voice muffled from all of Lucy's abundant locks.

Lucy chuckled, hugging her tighter before pulling back. "It is so good to see you. I cannot tell you enough how much I need you here. We have so much to discuss."

Evie cast a glance toward the house, linking arms with her sister. "I gather the duke is here now?"

Lucy nodded. "He is. They're in the drawing room having tea. I heard the carriage and said it would be you. They are waiting to see you. Mama is very pleased that you'll be home with us for some weeks."

"I'm pleased as well." They started toward the house,

entering the foyer where Evie gave a waiting-maid her pelisse and bonnet.

"Come, Evie, time to meet my betrothed."

"This is all so fast. I did not know he was even courting you." Evie watched Lucy and noted the light blush kissing her cheeks. Had the duke seduced her? She would not put it past the gentleman. His kissable lips were what made up women's fantasies in town.

"He arrived three weeks ago to call on Papa, something about land or some such, but it was during his time here that we were introduced. He was very kind and attentive and has been back often since then."

"So it's a love match then?" Evie asked, hoping that was true. The duke's reputation made it impossible not to judge and wonder if his motives were honorable.

"I like him very much. He's very kind. I think you'll like him too, Evie."

Evie didn't bother to mention that she already knew His Grace, no need muddying the water for something so small. In any case, he danced with many women in town. It was highly unlikely that he would remember her.

They walked into the front parlor, a small room, especially with her mother's crafts and knitting and her father's many books. The room was where they congregated most evenings before and after dinner, and it was nothing like the parlors of grand homes that dotted the English landscape. This one held few, and with the tall, dominating presence of the duke, the room appeared smaller still.

"Evie," her father said at the same time as her mama as she appeared. They both started toward her, arms outstretched and she hugged them both in turn. "We're so delighted you're home with us for some time. We've missed you, our dearest."

She smiled, pulling back from her mama and her comforting scent of lavender that always reminded Evie of home. "I'm happy to be home. I missed you all."

She glanced over and met the duke's calculating gaze. He was staring at her, and Evie looked back to her father to make the introductions.

"Oh, forgive me, my dear. May I present my eldest daughter, Miss Evie Milton. Evie, this is His Grace, the Duke of Carlisle. Lucy's betrothed."

Lucy blushed as she went to stand beside the duke, her shorter height against his taller frame making her appear even more dainty and delicate. Beautiful and perfect for him.

The duke bowed. "Miss Milton. How very good to see you again."

Evie dipped into a neat curtsy. "I… It is, Your Grace." She watched him a moment, and as if remembering his fiancée stood beside him, thrust out his arm for Lucy to place her hand atop his.

"How is London, Evie?" Lucy asked, bouncing beside her betrothed, her golden curls springing beside her face.

"Busy. Everyone who is everyone is in attendance. Molly and I have taken to riding in the park most days to keep our sanity. We've become excellent riders I think, much better than we used to be in any case."

"Oh, I do worry for you, my dear," her mama said. "Is Miss Sinclair still ensconced at Marchioness Ryley's former home?"

"She is, Mama," Evie said, talking of Willow's former companion who now chaperoned Evie and Molly about town. "I would not be able to stay there if not."

"That is very true," her father said, gesturing for her to sit before the fire.

Evie did as he bade and held her hands out toward the heat, grateful to be out of the carriage and home. She turned toward her sister and the duke, studying them as they too took their seats.

"I suppose congratulations are in order. I'm very happy for you, Lucy. Your Grace," Evie said. They were a strange pair, even if they portrayed or at least tried to portray otherwise. The duke sat as stiff as a rod beside her sister who, compared to him, was relaxed and bubbly as per her nature.

Maybe he liked women who were more outgoing than he was, although that went against everything that she knew about him. One would think that a consummate rake, a man who seduced the fairer sex with wicked intentions, would not look so uncomfortable with her sister.

Evie's eyes narrowed, taking in his features. Was he sweating?

"We're so pleased you'll be here for the nuptials, Evie. His Grace is going to have his good friend Marquess Ryley stand in for him, and I would like you by my side if you're willing."

Pleasure filled Evie at the thought of helping give away her sister on her big day. Even though there was a relative age difference between them, they had been close as children, and as all young women do, they dreamed of meeting their husbands and having a memorable wedding. "Of course. I would be honored." She glanced at the duke and tried to ignore his intense inspection upon her. Evie shot a look to Lucy, but her sister seemed oblivious to the duke's attention. Evie cleared her throat, unsure what the duke was about or why he found her so very interesting. Evie reached up to check that her hair had not slipped from its pins, or that her fichu was missing from her gown. No, all was in order. "Where is the wedding to take place?" she asked, wanting to remain engaged and excited about her sister's upcoming nuptials.

"At my estate," the duke said, cutting off her sister's reply. "The drawing room at Stoneheim Palace is very large and will accommodate the guests we intend to invite."

Evie adjusted her seat, warmer now. "I'm curious as to how you met. Will you tell me?"

"I had business with Mr. Milton and called one afternoon," the duke answered before anyone else could get a word in. "A delightful outing that turned even more so when I ran into your sister, Miss Milton. I asked to call again, and from there, we found we got along very well."

Lucy smiled at Evie, but there was something in her sister's eyes that gave her pause. The light within them was a little less bright when her betrothal was spoken of. Evie's eyes narrowed, and she wondered why that was. Outwardly her sister seemed happy and excited about the forthcoming marriage, but Evie wasn't convinced. She knew her sister better than anyone else in the world, and she wasn't as happy as she was pretending to be. Why, however, was the question.

"That is a lovely story. I'm very happy for you both." Evie smiled at her sister and promised herself when they were alone, she would ask that all was well. That her suspicions were incorrect, and her sister was merely nervous. To marry a duke was no small matter, especially to women such as themselves who may have a gentleman father, but little else to offer other than their person.

Lucy grinned. "I did not know you had met His Grace, Evie. How long have you both been acquainted?"

Evie looked to the duke as she tried to remember exactly when they met last.

"Midway through the last Season, I believe. I danced the cotillion with Miss Milton at the ball I hold annually in London."

Lucy's eyes widened at his exactness of detail and glanced between the duke and herself. Evie stared back, having not expected him to remember, certainly not to that detail. She knew she'd danced with him at his ball, but what that dance was precisely was lost on her. She had not thought he even remembered her name.

"I think you may be right, Your Grace. I admit you have a better memory than I," Evie said, making light of the situation.

"It was a pleasant spell about the dancefloor. One I will cherish always now that we're to be brother- and sister-in-law."

Lucy met Evie's eye, a question in her blue orbs. Evie shrugged, not knowing the duke remembered their dance so well.

Their mother cut in and started to discuss the weather and who would preside over the wedding, and Evie let the conversation flow over her. The duke and Lucy were a stunning pair, no matter that Lucy wasn't titled. She would have expected the duke to marry a lofty, titled woman, not a younger daughter of a penniless gentleman. But here they were, discussing invitations and where the happy couple would go on their wedding trip.

Evie listened and partook in the conversation when she could, but a part of her could not help but be a little jealous of her younger sister. At the age of seven and twenty, she had assumed to have been married and a mother by now. It wasn't so, and highly unlikely to occur now. But at least her sister would be happy, and that was a comfort at least.

~

$\mathcal{T}$he following day was a perfect summer day. Evie sat outside on a setting that looked out over her father's modest gardens. They were not as grand as the duke's at Stoneheim Palace, but then few places in England were as grand as his country seat.

Evie watched as the duke and Lucy strolled the gardens, every so often stopping to talk of a particular rose or tree. Her sister outwardly looked content and happy, but she was not at ease with the duke, and Evie couldn't help but wonder why. What was her sister hiding?

"Did you have any inkling at all, Mama that Lucy had feelings for the duke or that he, in turn, had feelings for her? We have never circulated with that family. Even I in London only really knew of the duke due to my friends and their elevated marriages. Do you not think Lucy may be a little out of step with him? Open to ridicule due to her lack of connections?"

Her mother finished her sip of tea before placing her cup down on the table before them.

"I did have my concerns, of course, regarding those matters, but I'm sure the duke is a good man and will not let Lucy suffer from any nastiness or jealousy that may arise at her lofty marriage accomplishment."

Evie didn't want to upset her mama and tell her that Lucy would be targeted and for quite some time by those in the *ton* who thought her marriage to the duke was above her reach. They would make her pay for marrying a man who only the worthy should have taken off the marriage mart.

"As for her feelings for the duke, I believe they like each other very much. I even hope that in time the duke will come to love our Lucy. I believe she already loves the duke."

Evie shot a look at her mama, not believing that for a moment. "Lucy loves the duke. Has she told you that?"

"Well, no," her mother said, casting a glance at her youngest daughter. "But look at her, the way she studies the duke, how she hangs on to his every word. Oh yes, I do believe she loves him very much."

"Mama," Evie said, her tone comforting, "I also look up at gentlemen when I speak to them, that does not mean that I'm in love with them. They have not known each other long, and I worry that Lucy may not like being a duchess. You know how much she loves her freedom, her life here in Wiltshire, and the people we know in Marlborough. She would not be able to circulate in that sphere any longer when she becomes the Duchess of Carlisle."

"Oh, the Duchess of Carlisle, how well that sounds, do you not think?"

"Mama," Evie chided. "Lucy will miss her friends. She has never tried to be anything more than what we were brought up to be. Daughters of an untitled gentleman with no dowry. Do you not think it's odd that the duke just arrived one day, supposedly regarding estate business and the next moment he's engaged to our Lucy? That is odd. I do not care how well Duchess Lucy sounds to you. I find it strange."

Her mama turned to her, reaching out to clasp her hand. "My dear, I know it is hard to see a younger sister wed before you, and to such a high position, but do please be happy for Lucy. She loves you so very much and will need your guidance and support during the next few weeks."

"I'm not jealous, Mama, if that is what you're implying. While I have hoped that marriage may become a possibility to me, something that is looking less and less an option at my age, I am happy for Lucy. I merely want to ensure that Lucy is satisfied and appeased. Once I'm certain of this, then I will throw myself into the wedding preparations with such enthusiasm that even you shall be sick of me."

Her mama laughed, and Evie smiled, but as she turned back to watch Lucy and the duke, the niggling doubt would not abate. Something was off. None of this hasty courtship made any sense, and she would satisfy her concerns before she allowed her little sister, someone she always promised to protect, to marry a man whom she did not love.

"Thank you, my dear," her mama said. "And do not despair. Now that your sister is marrying a duke, it is only a matter of time before a gentleman will wish to be associated with the Carlisle family and offer for your hand. This connection will throw you into the path of men of substance and breeding, I am sure."

"I do not think—"

"You will see, Evie," her mother said, cutting her off. "You too will be happily married by the end of next Season. The Duchess of Carlisle's sister cannot be a spinster."

Evie groaned, picking up a sugar biscuit and taking a substantial bite. "I never set out to be a spinster, Mama, as you well know, but neither will I allow anyone to parade me like a new, shiny goose ready to be plucked."

Her mama gasped, and Evie met her gaze, wanting her mother to know what she was implying. Just because her sister was to be a duchess did not mean anything. Not to society. Some of her closest friends were married, one to a duke, the others to a marquess and an earl. That had not changed Evie's or Molly's position. It simply gave them access to balls and parties that would otherwise be closed to them. No man of substance or breeding had bent the knee before her and offered for her hand simply because her friends were well placed in society.

It would be no different with her sister being a duchess. Having a sister so high on the social sphere did not change her circumstance. She was, after all, still a woman of no rank, no inheritance, and seven and twenty years. Gentlemen, unfortunately, were immune to seeing her or women like her for what they could give. A priceless prize worth so much more than anything else.

CHAPTER 3

*L*ater that evening, Evie sat in her room alone, brushing her hair. The door swung wide, revealing her discombobulated sister. "You have to help me, Evie," Lucy blurted as she stormed into her room, shutting and locking the door behind her. "I cannot marry the duke."

Evie stared at her sister a moment in horror. Had she gone mad since she'd left her in the drawing room, not an hour before with her family? "What! Why ever not?"

Lucy came over to where she sat before the fire, drying her hair after washing it. Her sister slumped onto the chair across from her, her cheeks and lips a ghostly white. "He arrived here not a month ago and has courted me ever since. Mama was so very pleased and happy that I did not want to upset her. You know she's not been well these past months, and it was nice to see her animated again."

"Mother has been ill?" Evie had not known that. Why did she not know that? "She never wrote to me about such a thing. I hope it's nothing serious."

Lucy frowned, marring her otherwise perfect forehead.

"I do not believe so. I think a lot of mother's forlorn countenance has something to do with Papa not wanting to travel to Bath this Season. In any case, she was happy and lively, and the duke was attentive and kind, and before I knew it, he was bowing before me and asking me to be his wife."

Evie sighed. It was just like her sister to get herself into such a pickle. "You did not have to say yes, Lucy."

Lucy made a sound representing an injured dog. "I know I did not have to say yes," she moaned, "but I felt compelled. He's so wealthy and powerful. He owns most of the land surrounding Papa's estate. I did not want to offend him, and I just blurted yes before I thought about it. But I cannot marry him. I don't want to be a duchess."

Evie snorted, unable to believe such a thing. Women in town would do almost anything to wear a ducal coronet atop their heads, but then this was Lucy, and she had never cared for such things. "There are very few who would not want to be a duchess. Are you sure you're not the one who is ill?"

"This is not a jest, Evie. I cannot marry the duke because, well, because I'm already in love with someone else."

"What!" Evie shot to her feet, the brush in her lap clanging onto the floor. "You cannot be in love with another man and have given your hand to the duke. Whatever were you thinking, Lucy?"

Lucy stood and started to pace back and forth from the bed to the fire. Her fisted hands at her sides telling Evie that her sister was upset and unsure of what to do. Evie took a calming breath, needing a clear mind to think about what was to be done.

"If you remember last year, Mama took me to Gretna

to visit her cousin. What she does not know was that I was seeing Mr. Anthony Brown, you know, the gentleman farmer on the other side of Marlborough. He's been courting me for some months and Evie," Lucy said, coming over to her and clasping her hands, "I love him so very much. He is everything that I've ever wanted, and when I'm with him, I care for nothing else."

"You've lain with him?" Evie shut her mouth with a snap, knowing she was gaping at her sister. How and when had all of this occurred? And how did she not know of it? She should have been here for her sister. To guide and help her through this. Although father would not have wanted either of them to marry a farmer, if he had seen his daughter's happiness with the gentleman, he may have relented. Neither of their parents was hard or so unforgiving.

"No, of course not. Mr. Brown is a gentleman, but I do wish to be his wife and he has asked for my hand. Secretly of course, no one can know of our love as yet. Papa will never approve." Her sister sat again, clasping her hands in her lap. "I will admit to kissing Anthony, but nothing more. I promise you."

That was something, Evie supposed.

"So you see, I cannot marry the duke, and if Anthony finds out that I agreed to marry the Duke of Carlisle as well he'll never forgive me. Father is going to have the banns called. My life will be over if I lose Anthony. Please, Evie. Please help me."

Evie bit her lip, at a loss as to what to do. What did one do in situations like these? Her mind jumped from idea to idea, each one dismissed as soon as she had it. The only thing left to do was tell the truth, no matter how difficult that may be. "You will have to tell Mama and Papa the truth and break off the understanding with His Grace. That is your only choice."

"No," Lucy gasped, her hand rushing up to her neck. "I'll be ruined if I do that. The whole town will think me a scheming minx with no regard to the duke. When they find out that Mr. Brown was already my betrothed, they will shun and hate me. The duke may be so enraged that he may try to injure father financially to seek revenge. No, no one must know that it was me who cried off. We need to keep father from posting the banns, and you need to seduce the duke into thinking he's asked the wrong sister to marry."

"Me?" Evie asked, pointing at herself. "I cannot seduce a duke. I'll be ruined. Think for a moment of what you're asking, Lucy."

"You're a confirmed spinster. I did not think you would mind."

Anger replaced the compassion she had for her sibling. "I may be unmarried, but I'm not a whore who'll ply her trade to repair an error that is of someone else's making. You need to tell the truth. You're the one who lied to both men. You need to make this right."

Lucy kneeled before her chair, clasping Evie's hands. "I'm sorry, Evie. I'm desperate. Please, please help me," her sister begged, gripping her hands tighter.

Evie shook her head, staring at her sibling, whom she had started to wonder if she knew at all. Whatever was she thinking about, getting herself into such a lie? "I wouldn't know the first thing about how to steal him away from you, and he's asked you to marry him. He likes you, not me. That idea will never work. You must own this mistake, I'm afraid."

"You're far prettier than I am. It'll be no problem at

all. Just show him more attention than I will. I'll distance myself over the coming days, be unavailable or away whenever he calls, and you shall take my place. He only ever talks in any case, he has not tried to kiss me, thankfully, and he's boring." Her sister pursed her lips, turning her head in thought. "London gossip paints him as a libertine, a rogue, and yet I do not believe it. He's never tried once to seduce me. I'm sure, though, he'd try and kiss you. As I said, you're much prettier than me."

The idea of the duke kissing Evie made heat pool at her core, and she slumped back onto the chair, her stomach in knots. "If I try and steal him away, he'll think the worst of me. No one does such a thing to a sister, and he's a gentleman, he would not do that to his betrothed."

"No, no no no, he'll simply believe that the feelings he had for me were misplaced. As you said, you've met before. Surely you can work with that. He does not love me, that I do know, and so it won't be so awful for him in the end. You do not have to marry him, merely pull his attention away from me long enough that he'll decide to end the betrothal."

"But what if he then offers for me? As you said, I've resigned myself to my lot in life. I don't know if I could marry a man who could be so fickle with his feelings."

"Evie, my actions toward the duke, my marriage, could ruin the family if he should find out. You need to make him turn his head toward you, fall in love with you if possible, but you need to do it soon. Please help me."

"Lucy," Evie sighed. "When is he to call next?" she asked, resigning herself to tell the duke the truth herself, no matter what Lucy wanted her to do. She could not seduce him. To do so was an abhorrent thought. Not because he was not deadly handsome, what with his chiseled jaw and straight, cutting nose, no. He was so very charming to look upon, but because she could not seduce a man away from her sister, even if asked to do so.

It was impossible to imagine, and he would question her loyalty toward her family if she tried such a thing.

He'd think her a horrible person.

And she would be a horrible person. No, she would tell the duke the truth and have Lucy own her mistake. It was what was best for the family. The duke would surely understand. As Lucy said herself, they hardly knew each other. It wasn't like their marriage was a love match. All would work out, and tomorrow she would solve this problem, and they could all get back to their normal lives.

CHAPTER 4

Finn had ridden hard to make his afternoon call to Miss Lucy Milton. He'd been held up with his steward regarding a letter from his attorney who queried about his marriage. Namely, when it would take place and reminding him of the time restraint he had on his person.

He pulled his mount up before the sandstone, modest estate, and sighed, running a hand across his jaw. What was he doing? He was marrying a woman whom he did not love and all for the sake of money.

Granted, it was a lot of money, and funds that were required to keep his many estates and the people who relied on him for a living. Even so, the thought of marrying a woman he did not care for grated on his conscience. Miss Lucy Milton was a delightful young woman, bright and happy, and seemingly very much in love with him. He ought to be satisfied he'd found a wife, a local girl who was not only the daughter of a gentleman but from his home county. Just as his father decreed in his will, but he was not.

He didn't love her past that of a passing acquaintance, no more than a friend.

The image of Miss Evie Milton flittered through his mind, and his blood stirred. He'd not thought to see her so soon, having expected her to stay in London. The fact that she'd returned home early to partake in her sister's wedding preparations hadn't occurred to him.

Stupid mistake and now one that haunted his dreams.

Evie was a little older than Lucy. Part of a friend set of some of the most powerful and influential women in the *ton*. And damn it all to hell, she was beautiful. Had she been a little younger, he would've courted her instead of her sister, but she was nearly thirty by his calculations—her breeding years long behind her.

She was not for him.

He needed a wife who would give him sons. A young wife was more suitable for that position. If he had to marry at all, he at least would ensure he had children and soon. To have an heir would at least be one thing less that he had to concern himself.

Finn jumped down and handed his horse to a waiting stable lad, throwing the boy a ha'penny for his trouble. The boy thanked him profusely, and Finn walked to the door, steeling himself to act the besotted fiancée that he was anything but.

The door opened, and he glanced up, expecting to see the young footman who also served as the butler. The person before him was most certainly not a man. Miss Evie Milton was all woman. Voluptuous, and curved in all the right places. His hands started to sweat in his gloves at the thought of running them over every portion of her body he could. Her cheeks reddened, her eyes wide and bright, and he steeled himself not to act the rogue he was rumored to be, and drag her up against him to kiss her soundly. Take those full lips and meld them with his.

Finn swallowed, remembering to bow. "Miss Milton, good afternoon. I hope I find you well today."

She stared down her nose at him, her gaze sliding over him like a caress. He shouldn't be reacting to her in this way. She wasn't for him, and yet, there was something about Miss Milton that made his blood burn. Had always made him burn even when he'd promised to never act the cad like his sire. He could only guess how many bastards lay littered about London his father had produced before his death last year.

"Your Grace, how very opportune this is for me. I was just about to go for a walk to ensure that my dog is well. She is expecting, you see. Perhaps you'd like to join me," she asked him, stepping down onto the lower step and closing the door at her back.

Finn ought to move aside to give her space, but he couldn't budge a foot. He was a bastard and one who may be more like his father than he wanted. "I thank you for the offer, but I must make my addresses to your parents and Miss Lucy."

"Oh, they're not home at present. Lucy wished to visit Marlborough, something about acquiring a new hat and traveling case, I believe. So, you see, it's only me here today."

She slipped past him with little care as to whether he was following her or not. The sound of her footsteps on the graveled drive loud in his ears as she walked away. Finn stood there a minute, debating his choices and decided a walk would do well enough so long as they stayed within the grounds of the house and were in view of the home. Her lack of chaperone could be overlooked.

"Very well, I shall join you, Miss Milton."

She stopped and turned, pulling a loose bit of hair out of her eye that had slipped across her face. Finn swallowed. The action should not be seductive at all, nor fill him with a longing to be the one to slip the stray piece of hair behind her ear, but it was.

He was the worst type of fiend and ought to be horse-whipped thinking of his betrothed's sister in such a way. He'd had the opportunity last year in town to court Miss Milton, and he'd chosen not to. Marriage had not been a thought to trouble him with. Stupidly he'd imagined he had time to choose a wife. While their dance had been memorable, to him at least, it had not caused him to lose his head and declare undying love.

Rallying himself to control wayward thoughts, he clasped his hands behind his back and raised his chin, all seriousness for their stroll about the garden. A damned hard feat when Miss Milton strode purposefully down the drive, heading out of sight of the home and at a pace that made it impossible to continue his sedate stride he'd started with.

"What is the rush?" he asked, catching up next to her. A light blush stole over her cheeks, and she pointed ahead of her.

"My wolfhound is in labor, or so Ben our gardener said this morning, and I want to be with her."

"You have a wolfhound?" Finn asked, his steps faltering. He wasn't an enthusiast of the canine breed, never trusting the beasts. Small dogs he could tolerate, but a wolfhound, those things were as beastly as they came.

"I do," she said, gifting him with a smile. "Her name is Sugar."

Sugar? His lips twitched at the farcical name, and yet he continued to walk with her, curious now to see Miss Milton's pet. "I'm hoping this Sugar is friendly."

"Oh, yes. Sugar has the sweetest temperament. She'll be fine with you since you're with me, she'll have no reason to distrust you. Normally she would be with me in the house, but due to her condition, Mama wouldn't let her stay inside until she'd had her pups."

"You allow the dog to live inside your home?" Pets were nonexistent in his life growing up. They had the odd barn cat, but they were wild and would leave a respectable scratch if anyone ever tried to catch them. As for dogs, his father had loathed them. Horses were the only animals allowed, and only because they served a purpose.

"Of course. Sugar sleeps on my bed whenever I'm home, and I miss her, but I'm also very excited to see her pups." She studied him a moment, working her bottom lip between her teeth, and the sight of it sent a bolt of desire to his cock. He clamped his jaw, looking away to remedy his nonsense. What on earth was wrong with him? He'd been away from town too long, and the bed of willing women, or he'd liked Miss Milton more than he'd admitted to himself. Not a helpful revelation since he was about to marry her sister.

"You never had pets as a child, did you, Your Grace?"

He kept his attention straight ahead and spotted a kennel of some sort near a small cottage. "You're very astute, Miss Milton."

"We have mutual friends, Your Grace. I do know you a little. Talking of such, would you like to call me Evie? I do prefer it to Miss Milton."

Pleasure thrummed through him at the thought of such a thing, but he couldn't allow it. Not until he'd married Miss Lucy, then he could be on more familiar terms with Miss Milton. Until then, he would not be calling her by her given name. "I think it would be best to remain Miss Milton and Your Grace if you do not mind. When I marry Miss Lucy, then I believe we may be on more familiar terms."

"Out of curiosity, however, what is your first name, Your Grace? If you're willing to disclose that, of course."

He cleared his throat, not sure he ought to tell her. To do so really defeated the purpose of his rule only a moment before. "Finlay, but close acquaintances call me Finn."

"I must admit," she said, chuckling a little. The sound as sweet as any he'd ever heard. He shouldn't find it so very carefree and relaxing to be around Miss Milton, and yet he did. More so than when he was with his betrothed. It was blasted inconvenient, and not to mention wrong. "I imagined a much more severe, stern type of name for a duke."

"My mother named me," he said without thinking. He rarely spoke of his mama, whom he'd lost when he was young. To think of her always made him melancholy, and yet, with Miss Milton, he seemed to be able to talk of the one parent who showed affection for the short amount of years that he had with her with no melancholy at all. Only pride and love.

"What name do you suppose a duke should have, Miss Milton? I'm curious to know."

"Hmm," She threw him a teasing glance and continued toward the kennel. "I do not know. I suppose perhaps George or Arthur, or even William. Finlay seems a carefree, happy type of name. I think it suits you," she said, meeting his gaze.

He smiled despite himself, enjoying this little stroll, not to mention her. He was enjoying her so very much as well. More so than he'd enjoyed his many strolls with Miss Lucy Milton. When he'd gone on walks with his betrothed, they would often go minutes at a time without speaking, and sometimes, Finn had to wrack his brain to think of things to talk about. The conversation did not come easy with Miss Lucy. He'd put it down to her being a little shy around him, he was a duke after all, and often brought on such reactions when around the fairer sex. Miss Milton, however, seemed to be a paradox.

Evie was easy to speak to, and a little niggling doubt crept into his mind that he'd made a mistake in choosing the younger sister. That he should have taken more time to see who would suit him as a wife. Instead, he panicked and picked the first gentleman's daughter in his home country who was appropriate. The debate on the matter reminded him why he'd dismissed Miss Milton in the first place. She was mature of age to be an agreeable wife. He needed a bride who would give him heirs. Miss Lucy would fill the role well. She still had ample years ahead of her to provide him with children.

By the time they arrived at the kennel, a man that Miss Milton introduced as Ben was waiting for them. From his worn clothing, dusted with mud and grime, Finn marked him as the gardener whom she had mentioned before.

Miss Milton went into the kennel, large and under-cover, and Finn followed at a slower pace, not wanting to stress the dog at his presence. The enclosure was large, needed to be for a wolfhound, and the brown-haired dog lay on a bed of straw, four little pups suckling milk already from their mother.

"She's had them already," he said, kneeling beside Miss Milton, keeping his hands well away from the dog or her puppies.

Miss Milton did not. She slumped onto the floor beside Sugar's head, patting her face and leaning down to kiss her head before she reached out and ran one finger over the new puppies' backs. An adoring smile slipped onto her lips, and something inside Finn ached.

What it would be like to be looked upon in such a way. With utter adoration and love. He supposed it was similar to what occurred when a woman had a child of her own. Unconditional love for her offspring the moment she saw her new babe. His father had not cared for him at all. His main priority was who his next bedding partner was to be. His son was the least of his troubles, so long as he was home, healthy, and out of the way, his father was content.

"Let Sugar smell you, and then you can probably sit closer if you like. She knows I'm relaxed with you, and so knows you are not here to harm her or her puppies."

Finn slowly placed the back of his hand near Sugar's nose, and she sniffed him a moment before lying back and putting her head on Miss Milton's lap. Having seemed to pass the little test, he sat on the straw bedding beside Miss Milton, merely watching the little puppies fight for a teat.

"They're charming, I will admit."

"When they're weaned, you may have one if you like. I have several friends who wanted a pup from Sugar when we bred her next, but I can hold one for you if you wish." She studied him a moment. Her head cocked a little to one side. "I can see you with such a grand dog. A duke should have a wolfhound."

He glanced at the puppies, having never given the idea much thought, even though he supposed he could have a pet if he wished. His father had not allowed them, but that did not mean that he could not do as he wanted now. Perhaps if he gave the canine breed a chance, he might like them better after all.

A novel thought and one he would consider.

"I shall ponder it," he found himself saying, reaching forward to run a finger across the back of a black pup that seemed eager for milk. "Do you think Sugar will have any more today?" he asked, having never seen a dog give birth before. That's what he told himself was the reason he wished to stay in this warm kennel, patting puppies. Though, he knew it was because he wanted to spend more time with Miss Milton, away from her family and society as they had been in London.

His good friend, the Duke of Whitstone spoke highly of her, and he could see why. She was no fuss, intelligent, and sweet. She adored her massive dog and cared for her sister and family. There was little one could not like about her.

The fact that she was beyond pretty also made his time with her easy. To look upon such beauty all day was never a chore.

～

*E*vie pulled the duke from the puppies after an hour of cooing, holding, and patting the adorable little mites before they returned to the house. Her family was due home at four, and it was well past three by the time they returned themselves to the house.

They sat in the front parlor, which gave Evie a view of

the front drive, taking tea and biscuits that cook had prepared for them on their return.

She studied him as she ate a slice of carrot cake. The Duke of Carlisle sat straight and tall in his chair, all proper again, no longer the relaxed nobleman she had talked to in the kennel only half an hour before.

How she supposed her sister thought that she would be able to seduce such a fine specimen of a man away from his beloved was an absurd notion. While they did get along, seemed on friendly terms, that did not mean he found her handsome as much as she found him.

Why she'd never even kissed a man before, so how was she going to seduce a seasoned rogue? It was an absurd notion that her sister even asked. No, if Lucy's happiness depended on breaking the understanding with the duke, then Lucy had to tell him the truth. Tell him that she loved another and would not marry him. That was the best course and the one Evie would make her walk when they returned home.

She frowned down in her tea. What would the duke do after the fact? Would he return to town? Marry a woman much closer to him in wealth and situation? The idea left a sour taste in her mouth, and she reached for more sugar to put in her tea.

"I thought to hold an engagement ball in some weeks. Do you think your sister would welcome such an event?"

The question brought her out of her dispirited thoughts and back to the duke. "I think she would like that very much," Evie lied, knowing her sister would hate that above anything else. To be paraded before all of the duke's closest friends as if she were in love with the man. No, she could not allow it to get that far. She would make Lucy put a stop to this madness.

33

"I shall need help in drawing up a list of guests to invite. Would you and Miss Lucy like to call on me tomorrow next, and we shall get a start?"

Evie placed her teacup down on the small table that separated them on the settees. "Perhaps we could join you for luncheon and start collating a list after that." Not that any lists or balls would be occurring. When Lucy returned home, the duke would be released from his offer, and everything would return to normal. Other than her sister marrying Mr. Brown that was.

"I think that will do very well." He threw her a small smile, his eyes lingering on her lips a moment before slipping away back to the biscuit he held in his hand.

A flutter of delight thrummed through her at his interest before the sound of carriage wheels on the drive outside caught her attention. Evie glanced at the window and spied her mother and father alight from the vehicle, her mother's countenance one of distress. Evie stood, the pit of her stomach tightening with impending doom.

Just as the front door swung wide, she met them in the foyer, leaving the duke alone in the drawing room.

"What has happened?" she asked her mother, whose face was pale, her eyes red-rimmed as if she'd been crying for a long time.

The absence of Lucy made her pause. "Is Lucy well, Mama? Where is she?" she asked, turning to her father, who merely stood looking at her as if he'd lost all sense and feeling.

"She's gone," her mama screeched, her eyes filling with tears and loud, wailing sobs filled the room.

"What do you mean she's gone? Tell me!" Evie demanded, shaking her father a little by his arm. "Father, tell me what happened." All terrible thoughts entered her mind that her sister had befallen a terrible accident and was no longer alive. Surely not. The idea did not bear thinking about.

"She's gone," her mother said again, more wailing that made Evie's legs start to shake that her little sister had indeed passed away.

"She's run off. With...with...Mr. Brown! You know, the farmer who lives west of Marlborough. Lucy asked to look at some cloth for a new dress, and I said that I would be along shortly as I had run into Ms. Oyster, my friend. I thought to meet her at the seamstress' store, run by Ms. Clay, but when I got there, not five minutes later, she was gone. The shopgirl handed me a missive. It was from Lucy and contained her apology and plans for her life."

"What did the note say exactly?" Evie asked, anger replacing her fear over what her sister had done. How could she do that to their parents, whom she knew would worry no end about her until they saw her again? As for Mr. Brown, he ought to know better than to act in such a selfish way. She would have some very stern words for him, too, when she met with him next.

"Not so very much. She asked us to notify the duke of her change of feelings and told us to release him from his duty to her. To marry another."

"I beg your pardon, Ms. Milton?" the duke said, striding from the drawing room, frowning down at her parents as if they were wayward children. "What has my betrothed happened to do?"

"It seems Lucy has run off, Your Grace. Run away to be married to a farmer we're acquainted with here in Marlborough. I'm very sorry," Evie said, turning back to her parents and leading her mama into the drawing room where she could sit. "At least Lucy intends to marry,

Mama. I'm sure all will be fine by the time she returns home."

"She's ruined herself, and for what? That Mr. Brown. He's a farmer, Evie. I had hoped that Lucy's esteemed marriage would help in settling your private circumstances, but it seems this will not be the case. Mr. Brown has no social standing, and you'll forever be an old maid."

Evie sat beside her mama, taking her hand to try to give comfort. The fact that the duke heard everything that her mama just said was mortifying enough than to make a scene about it. "You know I do not care about my circumstance in life. I shall get along well enough. Our concern now must be for Lucy."

"You're right," her mama said, clasping her arm. "We must hope she marries and is happy."

"What are you going to do about her actions?" the duke demanded, striding to stand before the fire and looking down at them all with displeasure. At some point, her father had also come into the room and sat on the settee aside them.

"We do not know where they have gone, Your Grace," her father said, his voice weary. "Lucy will return home when she's married, I believe. I see little point in chasing after her and making a scandal out of the situation."

"She's my betrothed. I suggest you ought to do a little more about it than that."

Evie rubbed her mama's back as the duke's words brought forth another bout of hysterics. "We are sorry for your loss, Your Grace, but there is little we can do, save going after her. She could be anywhere by now. Had run off in any direction. I'm sure in time, your heart will heal, and you'll marry again."

"That is what we shall do. Go after your sister and

inform her that she signed a contract to marry me, and she'll damn well abide by it, or I'll ruin your family even more than this escapade will."

"I beg your pardon?" her father said, standing and going forehead to nose with the duke, who was much taller than her sire.

Evie sighed. If her father meant to intimidate the duke, it did not seem to be working, if his thin lips and unimpressed glare were any indication.

"Apologies, Mr. Milton, but you were there when the contracts were signed. Contracts that bestowed upon you a large sum of money to ensure the marriage took place within sixty days. That money is now due since your daughter has run off with another man. So, unless you have that thousand pounds in your desk to reimburse me for my trouble, I suggest you do as I ask and go after your offspring."

"Father cannot travel far these days, Your Grace. His doctor has recommended he stay close to home," Evie said, feeling as though she needed to defend her parents, who were innocent as the duke in all this. Not that Lucy had told her of her latest plan. She had no idea that her sister would take such drastic action to end her betrothal. She was supposed to tell the duke the truth, not elope with Mr. Brown.

Oh dear, this was all such a mess.

"He has a bad heart," her mother said, hiccupping for effect.

The duke strode to the window, muttering under his breath before he turned, facing them all. His eyes were a little wild, and Evie shivered at the sight of him. When displeased, there was something oddly attractive about the man. He was much less refined, less the duke, and more the man.

A very delicious man who was once again free for the fairer sex to pursue.

He gestured toward Evie. "Your daughter will accompany me. To give Miss Lucy respectability when we return her home. They could not have gone far, and we shall return in a day or two."

"Evie is not going anywhere with you, Your Grace," her father said, his face going a little ruddy with his aggravation. Evie stood, going to him before leading him back to his chair.

"Sit, Father. You know the doctor said he did not want you to stress yourself in any way."

"You cannot go off with a man in a carriage. You'll be ruined, and then you'll never marry."

"I'll take Mary with me, and you forget that I'm already known in London as a spinster, Father. The duke will ride a horse outside the carriage, will you not, Your Grace?" she said, looking to the duke for agreement. "All proprieties will be met, I promise, should you allow me to go, that is."

Her father glanced at her mother a moment before his shoulders slumped, and he sighed. "Very well. You shall travel with the duke to fetch Lucy home. If you leave today, there is a chance you may catch them before nightfall." Her father clasped her arm, holding her firm. "She must not marry Mr. Brown, my dear," he whispered for her ears only. "I do not have the money to pay back the duke. Should Lucy marry Mr. Brown, it will ruin us financially, and we'll lose our home."

Evie sighed, her heart a little less full at her father's troubles. However, not all was lost. They shared mutual friends. Perhaps the duke could be persuaded to offer that money as a loan and allow her father to repay him over time should Lucy get her way and marry before they caught up to her. Evie could ask this of him. He was their neighbor after all in Wiltshire.

She nodded. "I shall, Papa," she whispered, before bidding them goodbye. She started for her room, needing to pack a valise and organize her maid Mary. There was much to do and very little time to do it in.

CHAPTER 5

he road toward London was arduous and lengthy, doubly so since she'd only just traveled it only two days before. Her maid sat across from her, her skin turning a darker shade of gray with each passing mile. It did not bode well for Mary being unwell so soon on the trip. They had many, many days ahead of them.

"Are you ill, Mary? You're quiet and pale," she asked, leaning forward to clasp Mary's hand, shaking it a little when she didn't respond. "Mary?"

The young woman leaned back against the squabs, taking a deep, calming breath. "Oh, Miss Milton, I feel so very poorly. I thought now that I'm one and twenty that my childhood traveling difficulty would have ceased to trouble me, but it has not."

"You feel as if you may be sick?" Evie asked, slipping to the side of the carriage to lower the window a little. They were traveling in the duke's carriage, a highly sprung, opulent equipage, and the last thing Evie wanted was to see Mary's stomach contents all over the floor or silk cushions. She doubted the duke would be appreciative of the gift.

"I do, miss." Mary curled forward, clasping her stomach. "Stop the carriage. Please, Miss Milton."

Evie yelled out to the driver through the window, and within a moment, the carriage rocked to a halt. No sooner had Mary stepped one foot outside did she cast up her accounts, only just missing her boots, but not, however, missing the duke's horse's hooves.

The horse stared down at Mary with a look of disdain, if horses were capable of such things. Mary was oblivious to all of them, merely continued to heave copious amounts of fluid all over the ground. Evie glanced up at the duke and noted he, too, had an inpatient, disdainful scowl across his brow that matched his horse.

Evie jumped down from the vehicle, going over to Mary and rubbing her back, giving comfort in any way she could. Thankfully she'd stopped heaving and was merely taking deep breaths, trying to calm her stomach.

"Do you feel a little better?" she asked, standing up and taking stock of where they were. Through the trees ahead, Evie spotted what looked like the start of their next town, Hungerford. On her way from London, they would typically change horses here, but they had not been traveling long from Marlborough. She supposed they could stop for luncheon, even though it was a little early for that.

"We shall walk into Hungerford. It is not far, and I think it's best that Mary doesn't get back into the carriage just yet. We could break our fast, which may help her unsettled stomach. Do you not agree, Your Grace?" she asked, catching his gaze.

His lips thinned, but he relented and nodded. "I agree. I shall ride ahead and order lunch for us all. Charlie," the duke said to the footman who sat at the back of the carriage, "walk with Miss Milton and Miss Mary to the Bear Inn. I shall meet you all there."

Evie helped Mary to walk toward the inn, and the closer they became to the town, the more the color appeared in Mary's cheeks. Her demeanor improved. Her eyes brightened, all good signs that a walk was just the thing to make Mary feel better. "I do believe the carriage was what made you unwell, Mary. We shall have lunch, and with any optimism, you'll be well enough to continue this afternoon toward London."

"I think I shall be well, Miss Milton. I'm so very sorry for being such an inconvenience. I thought my sickness whenever I traveled was past me. It seems it is not."

"No, and we didn't have time this morning to have a hearty breakfast before we left, so that may not have helped you at all, either." Evie spied the whitewashed inn in the bustling market town and started toward its front door. It was a large, coaching inn, many people bustled about it, and all of them looking very busy with their employment. A pretty bow window ran from the first to the second floor and made her think of Whites in London and its famous bow window.

The duke, who must have been watching them from indoors, stepped outside and into the sunshine, and a little flutter of pleasure settled in her stomach.

He was such a handsome man. Her sister was either addled of mind or she indeed was in love with Mr. Brown to have thrown a duke over for a farmer. Evie could not see herself parting from the duke should he offer for her hand. Had he chosen her to be his bride, she would've made him fall in love with her, no matter how long that may have taken. The duke watched them walk toward the inn, and

Evie shivered as his gaze took in her appearance, sliding over her like a caress. If he thought she had not noticed he was mistaken. There was little that she did not discern when it came to the duke.

Did he like what he saw? She supposed now that her sister had run off with another man, she no longer needed to worry about Lucy's plea for Evie to steal him away and force him to end their betrothal. Evie could only hope that her sister was married by the time they caught up with them. The duke may be disappointed for a time, but surely his heart would heal. That's if his heart was ever involved regarding her sister, and sometimes, the way he spoke and the way he looked at her, she could not help but doubt that was the case.

They came to stand before the duke, and he bowed, holding out his arm for Evie. "Miss Mary, you look much better already. Miss Milton, I have lunch served in the private parlor."

The inn inside was as busy as it was on the outside. The taproom was full of tables and people taking repast. Some sat at the bar, eating and drinking and busy discussing all sorts of matters while they waited for the next stagecoach or change of horses.

Her maid stared as if she'd never seen such a sight before, and Evie pulled her to where the duke was leading them. He opened a door and gestured for them to enter. The private parlor was a bright, airy room that overlooked the pretty River Dun. The table was full of bread and cold meats, cheese, and a steaming pot of tea.

Evie's mouth watered at the sight and she went forward, sitting down across from the window so she could watch the goings-on on the river. "This looks wonderful, Your Grace. Thank you for the delicious lunch."

He sat across from her, filling his plate with a selection of what lay before them. "Of course. It is no trouble."

Evie poured herself a cup of tea and sipping her dark brew, sighed in relief at having a cup. "How refreshing. I do not think I could survive without tea. Do you not agree, Mary?"

Mary giggled, and the duke smiled, cutting a large piece of cheese and placing it on his plate.

"I do not, Miss Milton."

"We're to travel to Reading next. It will be several hours in the carriage on rough, uneven roads I'm afraid. We will not make the next town until nightfall. Do you think you'll be well enough to continue, Miss Mary?"

"I believe so, Your Grace. Now that I'm having something to eat, all will be well, I'm sure."

~

*I*t was not the case. Finn stood beside his horse, who grazed the grass at the side of the road while Miss Mary heaved up her luncheon for the third time in as many minutes. Not a mile up the road and the carriage stopped so the maid could be sick. It wasn't to be borne, and it would not be able to continue. If he were to catch up to Miss Lucy Milton before she eloped with her preferred gentleman admirer, they had to travel swift and without issue.

He needed to marry Lucy. And he needed to marry her soon before he ran out of time and lost all his wealth to his cousin, bar his estate.

Impatience ate at him, and he sighed, his mind furiously working with what to do. "That's it. This cannot continue.

Miss Milton, you shall ride behind me on my horse until we reach Reading. Dickens and Charlie will escort Miss Mary back to Hungerford in the carriage and organize a private carriage to return her home to Marlborough. It is obvious that she will be unable to travel the full distance to London, nevertheless Gretna, should we need to go that far. I do apologize, Miss Milton, but we cannot dally any longer."

"But I'll be unchaperoned," Miss Milton said, her eyes wide with scandal.

She would be, unfortunately, but there was little he could do about it. The maid could not travel with them. Her stomach was not built for long distances, obviously. "We will go as brother and sister until London, and from there, we will take an unmarked carriage north to stop curious eyes.

"Dickens," he said, turning to his driver. "We shall wait for you in Reading."

"Right ye are, Your Grace," Dickens said, climbing back up onto the box.

"How long do you think we'll be in Reading? What if we run into someone we know? I'll be ruined."

"It is a risk we must take to bring back your sister. I'm sorry, but my mind is made up."

Miss Milton's lush mouth thinned into a displeased line before she turned to Mary, taking her maid's hands. She was very kind to her lady's maid, talking to her more as an equal than a woman who was her servant. As a duke, he'd never much thought about the people who worked for him, so long as they went about their duties and acted acceptably due to their position in a ducal household. He was always fair and kind, but not friendly. It was a novel thing to see.

"What are your thoughts, Mary? Are you happy with this plan?"

Mary nodded, her hair falling out of her many pins after a day of casting up her accounts. "I cannot continue, Miss Milton. I'm so very sorry to do this to you."

Miss Milton helped Mary back toward the carriage, her hand idly rubbing the maid's back in comfort. "It'll be well, Mary. I just hope that the ride back home is not too taxing for you."

"As do I," Mary said, stepping up in the equipage. "Thank you, Miss Milton. Your Grace," the maid said, before leaning back on the squabs and closing her eyes.

"Ensure Miss Mary is safely stowed on a private carriage back to Miss Milton's estate. Pay handsomely that should she need to stop, that the driver does so whenever required. We shall meet you at Reading tomorrow."

"Very good, Your Grace," the driver said, clicking the reins to turn the equipage about, before they started back down the road they'd just traveled.

"Come, Miss Milton," Finn said, holding out his hand to help her up onto his horse. She cast him a glance, taking in his horse, and her eyes widened. No doubt the idea of riding his high beast and traveling all the way to Reading the least of her desires.

She turned and waved the carriage away and then did as he bade, striding over to him and holding out her hand for him to clasp.

The moment he wrapped his fingers about her own, heat crept up his arm and into his chest. He heaved her onto his horse, wrapping her hands about his stomach and securing them before him. It was not necessary that she hold him so tight, but against his better judgment, he helped her to. She leaned into his back, hugging him tight and the feel of her legs, her arms wrapped about him, made his mind seize with notions. Other imaginings of them together, wrapped close and tight.

He closed his eyes, steeling himself for the long-spun afternoon ride to Reading. Without further ado, he turned his mount and kicked it into a canter, needing to distract himself from the woman behind him. Finn soon realized his mistake of placing Evie behind him. She undulated against his back with every step, and he now knew the feel of her breasts. Soft and full and not his to touch.

He was marrying someone else, he reminded himself. The woman behind him was his betrothed's sister. She was prohibited to him.

The hours loomed ahead of him. Hours of torture mixed with pleasure.

He would not survive it, of that he was certain.

CHAPTER 6

*E*vie's bottom had gone numb hours before, and she was no longer aware of her legs. They too ached, and with every step of the horse's hooves, she cringed, wanting to get off the beast and never, ever to get on another one.

To ride so many hours when one was not used to the exercise was not to be borne. An outing around Hyde Park was one thing, but miles on the back of a horse, over uneven, slippery, and sometimes rocky terrain was quite another. She would be thankful for the carriage again tomorrow, and not only because her bottom would thank her for it. She questioned she could last another day seated behind the Duke of Carlisle without her hands doing something uncomely, like caress his chest.

She glanced over his shoulder, her eyes moving to take in his profile. For all the pain her bottom was currently experiencing, her body suffered nothing but pleasure. One that the duke wrought within her.

He was so very fetching. His straight nose and chiseled jaw and sweet-looking lips left her breathless and aching

48

and not just her behind. The idea that should her sister's plan to marry another be thwarted and the duke became her brother in law, Evie knew she would have to limit her time with her sibling from the day of their marriage.

There was something about the duke that she liked, and deep down, wanted for herself. Silly of her, really, as she'd never thought too much about him when they were in London and circulating within the same set of friends. But now, out in the country and headed toward London, there was little else to imagine. It was all she thought about.

Evie flexed her hands, feeling the hard, muscular lines beneath her fingers before clasping them together to stop her inappropriate caress. He stilled at her touch, something he'd done often during the trip north. Her breasts felt heavy in her traveling gown; her nipples hardened points from slipping against his back. For a time, she'd leaned her head against his spine, merely trying to grapple with the pleasures she was taking from the duke while she could.

He was so overwhelming that if they did not stop soon, she would be tempted to rub up against him like a cat seeking a satisfying pet.

A carriage rumbled past them, and Evie glanced ahead to see the beginnings of a substantial village. Relief poured through her that she'd been soon on her feet. For all the delightful reactions that the duke brought forth within her, she would be thankful to stand.

Within a short amount of time, the duke pulled up his horse before the Crown Inn, a redbrick building with a stable yard to one side. He reached around, holding out his arm. "Here, let me help you down," he said, meeting her gaze.

Evie diverted her attention to his hand and clasped it

tightly. Why did he have to be so consuming? So generous and charming?

So unavailable.

Well, at least in his opinion, he was. He was right at this moment, chasing after her sister to beg her to marry him still, even though she was in love with someone else.

The thought of him doing all that he had set out to achieve filled her with despair, and she slipped from the horse. She had expected her legs to hold her upright, but instead, her knees gave way, and she continued her downward spiral until her bottom hit the dirt and rocky courtyard.

"Miss Milton," the duke shouted, jumping from his mount and bending down to assist her. He clasped her hands and helped her to stand.

"Thank you, Your Grace," she said, reaching behind her and trying to massage her bottom without being apparent to those around them. "I seem to have sat too long today."

The duke frowned down at her, all seriousness. "I should have asked if you were accustomed to such lengthy rides. I apologize for the lapse in care, Miss Milton."

"Evie, please. Miss Milton makes me sound like a spinster."

He threw her a small smile, before handing his horse to a waiting stable lad and leading her indoors. "You may call me Finn then in return. Especially since we're to be brother and sister for a time."

"That is true," she said, returning his smile before taking his arm.

They headed inside the inn and stopped in the taproom. It, too, was similar to the one they had luncheoned at earlier today in Hungerford.

"Two of your best rooms, if you please. For one night."

The publican rubbed his hands down his grimy apron and studied them both. "I only have one room left. 'Tis the best I have." The publican's eyes narrowed on Evie, and she stepped closer to the duke, hiding a little behind his arm.

"My sister and I need separate rooms. I will pay handsomely."

The man shrugged, crossing his arms across his broad chest. "Canna help ye, I'm sorry. I ave one room. Take it or leave it."

Evie glanced at the duke and didn't miss the pained expression that crossed his features. She supposed it wasn't her he wanted to be alone with but her sister. No matter what Lucy thought of the duke, Evie had no idea if his feelings were genuine. Everything that she'd seen of him when around her sibling told her they were.

Perhaps he was heartbroken that her sister had run off with another man.

"We'll take the room," he said, his voice bored. "Have a maid bring up a hip bath for my sister, and we'll be looking for a substantial dinner, with wine. Also, extra bedding as I'll be sleeping on the floor."

The publican's eyes brightened, sensing the man before him was of some means. "I canna bring up a mattress that we have spare if ye would like. Ye may place it before the fire to keep warm."

"That will do very well. Thank you."

The man bellowed out for a Masie, and a young, disheveled woman ran into the taproom, her cheeks ruddy from exhaustion, a small line of sweat across her brow.

"Take the gentleman and his sister up to our best room and then come back to me for further instruction."

The young woman bobbed a curtsy and gestured for them to follow. "Of course, Papa." She took in their appearance and then gestured for them to follow. "This way, if you please."

They climbed a short flight of stairs and walked along a narrow passageway before Maisie unlocked a door and pushed it wide, showing off their best bedchamber for their guests. The room had a stoked fire set and ready for the next guests to occupy the space. The maid quickly went over to it, and using a tinder box lit the kindling.

Two chairs sat before the hearth. A large, wooden bed lay in the middle of the room and beyond that a small antechamber with a door. Evie walked over to inspect where the door led and found a water closet and small hip bath inside. Evie supposed they at least could bathe and take care of their personal needs without the other hearing and seeing anything.

A small mercy since they had to share the same chamber.

Evie waited at the end of the bed until the maid left. The moment the door closed behind the servant, she went over and pulled the bedding back, checking the sheets for lice. The bedding was clean and smelled of lemon and was thankfully free of bugs.

"You may have the bed. I'll sleep before the fire on the mattress they're bringing up."

She strolled about the room, looking out the bank of windows that overlooked the main thoroughfare of the town, the bustling carriages, and people. Had her sister even traveled through here on her way to London? Did they go to London first, or did they travel north by some other means? Their journey north may be a waste of everyone's time, especially if Lucy was already married to her Mr. Brown. Or worse, was hiding somewhere like Bath.

Movement out the corner of her eye caught her attention, and she turned to see the duke pulling his shirt up over his head, throwing it haphazardly on top of the wingback chair before the now-crackling fire. His cravat, waistcoat, and coat already discarded.

Her mouth dried at the sight of his chiseled body. Never before had she seen a man in such a near-naked state. Her fingers itched to run down the center of his chest, the slight decline that pointed toward his breeches a road she'd certainly like to travel. She bit her lip, all delicious, wicked thoughts entering her head. What would his skin taste like if her tongue was to poke out and lick it? Was the modicum of chest hair coarse? Would it tickle her face if she were to lay her head against him?

Evie turned to look out the window. Wherever did that thought come from? She shut her eyes a moment, disgusted at herself for the wayward contemplation. If he caught her ogling him, the spinster sister of his betrothed, it would not be borne. No matter how much she may wish to be of interest to him, she could not be. He was meant for another, and she would have to remember that until she saw her sister was indeed married and happy with her choice.

The realization struck her mute, and she stared out the window, wondering what she would do about the truth. Her sister had asked her to help break off the understanding, but to do so without him knowing that Lucy was in favor of this plan made her look like an evil, villainous sister.

But then, he was aware that her sister had run off with another man, so he must at least have had the thought that

Lucy did not want him as he'd hoped. Not that Evie dreamed of marrying the duke herself, but she certainly wouldn't mind a stolen kiss or two from the handsome beast. And if that kiss led to more, or they found that they suited better than he did with her sister, there was nothing wrong with that. Indeed, never before had her stomach fluttered, or her heart raced as much as it did when she was around His Grace.

The very sight of him without his shirt had made her ache in places she hadn't known could and made her long for things she'd thought lost to her. Maybe her sister running off and breaking her betrothal was a sign, a possibility that Evie may have a chance at happiness after all.

She stole a glimpse of the duke, who was now hunting through his traveling bag, looking perhaps for a change of clothes. All of this, however, depended on whether he saw her in a romantic light, which at present, she did not think he did.

"I'm going to go wash up," he said, striding past her as if walking about half-naked in a room with a woman who was not his wife was a natural occurrence.

The rogue...

A knock sounded at the door, and Evie bade the maid enter. Two burly men brought in hot buckets of water that they placed near the entrance to the water closet, along with a hearty meal and wine that they set up on a small table before the fire.

"We'll be back in an hour to clean away the dishes and to make up the second bed," the maid said, bobbing a quick curtsy before leaving.

Evie sat before the fire and poured two glasses of wine, the smell of lamb and vegetables making her stomach rumble. The duke joined her, dressed appropriately once more, but still as handsome as sin.

A self-satisfied growl left his lips at the sight of the food, and she fought not to react to the sound. She was not herself with him. Never before had she reacted in such a way to a man, so why was she doing so with the duke? When in London she hadn't crooned like a besotted debutante when dancing with him, but then in London they had not been alone, and she had been only too busy trying to remember the steps of their dance than worrying about what he thought of her. If at all.

"I'm ravenous," he said, smiling at her as he took a sip of his wine.

Evie knew the feeling well and not always for the food that was before her. She nodded, smiling. "The stew and bread do smell delicious. Thank you for all of this, Finn. I shall repay you my fare to London when I'm able. I apologize that my father was unable to before we departed."

"I understand your father's predicament. This is not a mammoth expense. I think I can withstand a few days on the road with my *sister*," he said, his mouth twisting into a wicked grin.

Evie chuckled at his remark against their lie to the landlord of the inn that they were related. She picked up her fork, stabbing at a potato. The stew burst a kaleidoscope of flavor onto her tongue, the meat tender and flavorsome, the vegetables cooked to perfection, and not overdone. The bread hot and spiced. The red wine complemented the lamb and left Evie's tired muscles soothed and relaxed as if she'd soaked in a deep, hot bath.

"I've never traveled to Scotland before. I just hope the carriage arrives by tomorrow, so I don't have to ride behind you again on your horse. I do not believe my body is capable of that many hours again on the back of your mount."

He smiled. "I do apologize again, Evie. I should have asked you if you were able to ride for such a distance. I will not make that mistake again."

She shrugged. One of the main reasons behind her discomfort was the fact that she'd had to hold on to him for so many hours. Even now, her fingers could feel the contours of his body, the heat from his skin, the smell of sandalwood, and clean, pressed linen. Now that she'd seen him without a shirt, well, that image was imprinted into her mind and didn't help her body recover from being pressed up hard against him for hours on end.

"Please do not feel as if you have to sleep on the floor on my account. The bed is large enough for both of us, and as you know, no one knows you or I here, even if caught together." Evie snapped her mouth shut, unsure where the scandalous thought came from. Or perhaps she did know. From years of wishing to find a husband like her friends had, who would love her as passionately and devotedly as they were. Her body, at times, physically ached with the need to have what they did. To be as happy as they were.

Even so, she and the duke could not share the same bed. The floor would have to do for him.

He shook his head, sipping his wine. "I cannot do that. You're an unmarried maid and my betrothed's sister. It would not be right."

Evie thought about his response. He needed to know that his chances of marrying Lucy were nil now that her sister had run away with another man. Surely, he could see that. "Lucy is probably married by now, and even if she isn't, surely you do not wish to marry a woman who is in love with someone else." The duke deserved happiness, like everyone else. There was no reason why he could not take his time in courting another and then marrying them. He was only young and had plenty of time to choose a bride.

"You do not know that she's married."

"No," she agreed, understanding too well that Lucy did not want to marry the duke even if there wasn't a Mr. Brown involved in her sister's elopement.

"Of course, I do not want to marry a woman who had thrown herself at someone else, but there are other things at play."

"What things?" Evie asked, studying him as he sat forward, adjusting his seat.

"Many things. Money has been changed hands between your father and myself. Marriage contracts have been signed."

All true, unfortunately, but even so, until the vows were spoken, no one was obligated to follow through on the agreement. "Lucy and Mr. Brown are a day ahead of us with travel. For all we know, they could have gone on horseback instead of a carriage, making them faster than we are in a carriage. He may have secured a special license, and they plan on marrying in London. You may be too late."

"I may be too late, but I have to try."

"Why?" Evie asked, curious now. He went to adjust his cravat that wasn't there, not after the stripping of his shirt earlier. Instead, his action brought her gaze to his neck and the shirt that was only partially buttoned. He had a lovely throat. She looked down at her meal, needing to distract her view of him.

"We had an agreement. I'm a duke. Who turns down being a duchess for heaven's sake?"

"Finn," she said, her tone a little chiding. "I feel I should warn you that should my sister still be unmarried by the time we meet with her, she may not wish to marry you, and I shall not force her. Nor will I allow you to do so." Especially when she knew that Lucy did not want to marry the duke at all. What a terrible mess this all was.

He stared at her a moment, his eyes narrowing. "I will not force her either, but I think I am owed an explanation and or at least an apology. I do not like scandal and strife. I've had enough of that to last me two lifetimes, and I will not see my name dragged down and gossiped about London as the latest *on dit*, all because of your sister's actions." He paused, wiping his mouth roughly with his napkin. "If she does not wish to marry me, I will ensure she is married, and therefore, my name cannot and will not be associated with her again."

Evie placed down her fork and leaned back in her chair, exhaustion swamping her all of a sudden. "I fear you may have no choice in that."

"I fear you are wrong," he said, digging back into his meal with gusto.

Evie stood, starting toward the private water closet they had. "I'm going to pour the buckets of hot water into the hip bath and freshen up."

"Oh, let me help you with those," he said, standing and striding toward the buckets before she had a chance of telling him she was more than capable. Evie stood back and watched as he poured the four buckets into the tub, the muscles on his back flexing whenever he bent over and tempting her yet again.

"Thank you." Evie stood aside as he passed.

"You're very welcome." He stopped beside her, and she looked up, meeting his deep-blue orbs that were heavy-lidded and made her skin prickle in awareness. "Enjoy your bath, Evie." His voice was deep and husky.

Evie forced her legs to move toward the room, but stopped at the threshold, throwing him a glance over her shoulder. "I shall...Finn."

CHAPTER 7

Finn was in hell. Literally. The sound of the hip bath water splashing in the adjacent room, the moans and sighs from Evie whenever she relaxed in the small tub was torture. His mind filled with images of her naked, sweet form, of her breasts turning into a rosy-pink hue from the warm water. Her skin supple and fragrant from the soap.

She would taste delicious, and he wanted to kiss every part of her. Fill himself with her flavor and gorge himself until he could not sustain any more.

He leaned forward on his chair, clasping his head in his hands. He was betrothed, damn it. He was supposed to marry Evie's sister.

The thought gave him pause. He was running out of time to court and marry anyone else from his home county. Not that he had many to choose from. Lucy Milton was the only one who suited his needs and his father's decree in his will. Young to bear children and born from a gentleman's family.

The elder Miss Milton could substitute for her younger

sister, he supposed, but she was much older. Less likely to give him sons. She was a spinster well on her way to sitting with the matrons of the *ton* each Season, watching over their young charges instead of being a new wife.

He sighed, hating the thought of Evie being shelved in such a way. She may not be suitable for him, a duke who needed healthy sons and soon, but she would be suitable for a rich gentleman, or even a lord.

In truth, he needed to think about what he would do should Lucy be married. Why she agreed to marry him in the first place if she was in love with someone else was beyond him, but that didn't matter now. If he could convince Miss Lucy to relent on her current course, return to Wiltshire and marry him instead, all would be well. Before his sixty days were up and he was left penniless. Not that the idea of marrying the chit filled him with any sense of expectation now. She'd made her choice, as absurd as it was, and she should live with it. No, he would ensure she was married so he could ask another to be his bride, return home and find one posthaste.

The door to the water closet opened, and Evie moved into the room. With each footstep, her shift swayed against her legs and gave him a delightful view of her ankles. She had donned a long dressing gown, giving her discretion, and yet, still, his blood heated at the sight of her.

Her hair was no longer pinned up but lay against her shoulders in dark, loose curls. Her lips pinkened from the bath, and her skin was glowing. He tore his gaze to the fire. He didn't need to look at her any more than he obliged to. She was too tempting, too sweet and innocent for him to be having such thoughts about her. Of what he'd like to do with her.

Of how he'd ravish those full lips, kiss her neck and

suckle upon breasts that would haunt his dreams from this night onward.

She sat in the chair across from him and unable to deny himself, he took his fill, from her bare feet to her delectable lips.

"Are you sure you wish to sleep on the floor? You are paying for the room. I feel bad for you having to sleep so rough."

At the mention of his bed that will be on the floor, a knock sounded on the door. Finn bade them enter and stood when a young manservant carried in a mattress, a maid following on his heels with linens and blankets.

"Here you are, sir," the maid said, helping the young man set up the bed before the hearth. Finn and Evie stood aside and watched as they quickly set the bed up on the floor. "Will there be anything else, sir?"

"No, that will be all. Thank you." He followed them to the door and threw the bolt across as their footsteps echoed down the hall.

Evie stared at his bed a moment before meeting his gaze. "Well, if you're sure then. Goodnight, Finn."

"Goodnight, Evie."

He didn't watch as she settled under the blankets or look to see when she fell asleep and rolled onto her back. At the sound of even, deep breaths, he took her in, a smile quirking his lips as he noticed that she slept in the center of the bed, one of her arms laying out to the side and taking up most of the spare room.

Finn sat for several more hours before the fire, watching as the wood turned to ash. He stoked it high for the night, before settling himself into his makeshift bed. Surprisingly it was warmer than he thought it would be, and yet sleep eluded him. The soft exhales coming from the other side of the room made him crave things he should not want, and it wasn't to be borne.

He was in hell.

*S*ometime in the middle of the night, Evie shivered awake. She sat up, groping to find her blankets that she had kicked off and that lay heaped at the end of the bed. The room was dark, save for the few slivers of moonlight that came in through the closed curtains.

She glanced toward where the duke slept, a mound before the fire that glowed with hot coals but no wood. Evie slipped out of bed, making her way carefully over to the fire. She picked up one of the coarse logs that were stacked neatly at one side and threw it on, the wood added to the hot coals sizzled and spat a moment before it caught alight and delightful heat chased the chill away.

Checking that the fire grate was in place, she tiptoed past the duke. For a time, she would sit in the chair and warm herself before returning to bed. There was a draft in the room and one that had chilled her to her bones.

Her foot caught on his mattress, and she tumbled, unable to right herself. Evie came down hard onto the duke, buffeting her fall with her hands as much as she could, even so, the feel of his solid, naked chest against her palms made her body burn. "I'm so sorry, Finn."

"What on earth are you doing?" he said, his words slurred with sleep.

She cringed, could just imagine what he was thinking. That she was throwing herself at him, quite literally. It was bad enough that she'd had thoughts to do precisely that, nevertheless doing so without his approval. "I was stoking the fire, and I tripped on your bedding. I do apologize."

His hands came around to settle on her waist, and he lifted her off him, setting her to one side of his bed. "Are you well? Did you hurt yourself when you fell?"

Only her pride. He probably thought she'd fallen on him on purpose to make him manhandle her. Heat bloomed on her cheeks, and she was thankful that the room was filled with shadows so he could not see her embarrassment. "I am well. I do apologize," she stammered, moving toward the side of the bed to go back to her own.

"Wait." His arms ran over hers, warming her more than any fire would. Evie stilled, biting back a sigh of pleasure at his touch. "Your skin is as cold as ice."

His statement pulled her from her thoughts. "That's why I came over to the fire. I was going to warm myself in a chair for a time."

He pushed down his blankets and patted the space beside him. "Come, lie by me. I'll keep you warm. No one will know, and no harm will come to your reputation. I promise you that."

She stared at the space beside him with longing. She would like nothing more than to be near the duke and all his sweet handsomeness, but she could not. To lie beside him was a temptation she did not think she could deny herself.

"I shouldn't." She hesitated, her voice breathless. There was no hope for her. Whenever she was around him, she acted like a silly little fool who was experiencing her first turn about a ballroom floor with a man.

"But you will." He clasped her hand, pulling her down

to lie beside him before righting the blankets to cover them both. His arm sneaked out about her waist, and he hoisted her up against his chest.

Evie stared into the darkness of the room, his chest a solid length of muscle against her back. Comforting warmth seeped into her chilled veins, and she could feel her eyes grow heavy with sleep even though her body thrummed with need.

She wiggled, getting comfortable, and his grip tightened. "Be still." His breath tickled her neck, and she bit her lip, tempted to wiggle some more to see what the duke would do.

"Sorry, I was trying to get comfortable." Evie fell to sleep with a grin on her lips.

⁓

*E*vie woke with a sense of contentment. Sometime during the night, she'd turned in the bed and was now draped over the duke. Her head lay nestled on his shoulder, her leg laying over one of his and her arm slumped across his chest where she could feel the steady beat of his heart.

She should move, slip out of bed, and dress, and yet she could not. She didn't want to. To lie in a man's arms, held tight against him in sleep was a delicious experience that she'd never had before. It was new and kind of lovely. Who would not like such a way to start the day?

He shifted a little beside her, pulling her close and laying a soft kiss atop her head before he stilled. Evie wondered at the unexpected gesture; sure he had not meant to kiss her.

"I do apologize, Evie. Sleep always makes me a little hazy come morning. I did not mean to accost you so."

She glanced up at him and met his gaze. Her heart beat a little faster in her chest at his heavy-lidded inspection of her. For the life of her, she could not move. If he were like any of the other gentleman who prowled the *ton*, surely he may lean down and kiss her? Make use of the opportunity when it arose. She wanted him to kiss her. Her first kiss and possibly her last ought to be with a man like the duke. If she were not ever kissed again in her life, at least she would have experienced one kiss with a man who she valued and liked.

He sighed, rolling onto his back to stare at the wooden-beamed ceiling before he left the bed, striding toward the chair where he'd left his clothing the night before.

His back flexed as he hastily pulled on his shirt, his waistcoat, and threw his cravat about his neck untied. "I'll go downstairs and order breakfast and check on the whereabouts of our carriage. I shall return presently."

Evie sat up, holding the blankets to her chest and stared at the door as it slammed closed, leaving her alone. Was his hasty exit due to his reaction to her? Reactions that he had not counted upon. They were going to be around each other for some time yet, weeks perhaps, if he became satisfied that Lucy was married and no scandal will darken his name, maybe he would look for another to be his wife. They certainly rubbed along well enough and had things in common, not wealth or connections, but where they were born, duty to do the right thing, and mutual friends. They suited better than the duke and Lucy did, at least Evie thought so.

What she felt whenever around the duke was new and nothing like the lackluster emotions that other men had produced in the past. Her body seemed to come alive, to yearn to be near him, to want to listen to his authoritative, commanding voice speak. The way he had held her last night and his impromptu kiss this morning had to mean something.

Did it not?

CHAPTER 8

*A*n hour later, after a hearty breakfast of bacon, ham, and coffee, they were on the road, heading toward Slough. He hoped they would make London by nightfall, especially now that upon entering the taproom, the landlord of the inn jovially notified him that their carriage would momentarily arrive.

Finn was thankful for it. He wasn't sure how he was going to survive another day with Evie behind him on the horse. Her chest bouncing up against his back, her hands slipping to sit at the tops of his breeches and making him wish her grip would move lower to caress him. The very thought of having her had filled his dreams, and he'd awoken unsure if his dreams had not come pleasantly true. Without thought, he had kissed her and pulled her into his arms like a lover after a good romp. Before sense had rocked him back into reality.

No, at least in the carriage, he would be able to think straight and keep a safe distance from the delectable Evie, who was not suitable as a bride, no matter how comely she was. A spinster well in the making who was past her childbearing years. If he was being forced into marriage, his wife must be a woman five years his junior at least and not the same age. Even a debutante would do if he could find one from Wiltshire and near his home in Marlborough.

They pulled out of the inn's yard and through the high street of the town. His betrothed had run off with another man, could be at this very moment married to Mr. Brown, ending his ability to marry her before his sixty-day deadline.

What to do? Should he continue north from London to chase down Miss Lucy, it would all but stop his ability from courting someone else in time to marry unless he threw away his conflicting thoughts on Lucy's sister and wooed Evie instead. He would seek out his doctor in London and ask him his opinion on older mothers and their ability to have children. The Duchess of Whitstone and the Countess Duncannon had both birthed children last year, and they were of the same age as Evie. Maybe her time to be a mother wasn't behind her after all.

Finn frowned down at the carriage floor, his gaze slipping to Evie's traveling boots, which were worn and in need of new soles. Each moment he was around Evie, he was tempted to ravish that pretty little mouth of hers. A mouth that occupied his thoughts more than Miss Lucy's had ever done so.

The carriage rumbled on the gravelly, uneven road, only the sound of the wheels on the ground and his driver talking to the accompanying footman could be heard. Evie was unusually quiet. A thick book open in her lap, and yet he'd not seen her turn a page for the past five minutes. He could not but wonder what she was thinking on, or pretending to read. Was she thinking of him? Finn inwardly groaned at the sight of her bottom lip clenched tight between her teeth in thought. Evie flummoxed him, tempted and intrigued him more than he was comfortable with.

How had he not noticed her in London these past years? Miss Milton had been no more than a passing acquaintance, a mutual friend through the Duke of Whitstone. A conundrum and a shameful one, really.

Because she wasn't high enough on the peerage ladder for you to look.

Finn ground his teeth at the little chiding voice that whispered in his mind. And the voice was right. He'd always planned to marry a woman of wealth and position and not anytime soon. He had his father to thank for rushing him to the altar. Evie and her sister were neither of those things, and yet his scandalous, nefarious father was no doubt laughing down on him, or up on him perhaps, at the position his son was now facing due to his own stupid will.

Now he had no other option but to marry a woman such as the Milton sisters.

Tonight they would reach London. It would be late, a fortunate occurrence, and one that should stop anyone from seeing them together and without a chaperone. They would break in London and head off for Gretna in an unmarked carriage. The less conspicuous they were on the road, the better.

Finn leaned back against the squabs, watching Evie. Warmth seeped into his bones on the chill morning at the thought of having her under his roof. He'd never had a woman sleep in his home before. Not since his mama was alive, at least.

Evie was a temptation he doubted he could ignore for long, and so it made sense to satisfy his father's will that his attentions would have to turn to the woman before him. There was no time left to find anyone else more suitable for his needs, and he liked Evie. She was sensible and beautiful, and as a duke, he could never marry someone who was nonsensical.

A short time later, his carriage pulled to the side of the road. Finn checked their location and in the distance could see Windsor Castle and Eton College nestled on the hills beyond. They were not far from Salt Hill.

The carriage dipped as his coachman climbed down from his box before he came up to the window. "The horses need a rest, Your Grace. This is a pretty view as any if ye wish to stroll for a time, break your fast with the picnic the innkeeper packed ye."

"Perhaps we should break for lunch, Your Grace? I am a little starved."

Finn glanced about and noted the open fields to both sides of the road and the forest that circled those fields farther away. "Of course," he said, opening the carriage door and stepping down. He turned and helped Evie outside, and the moment their hands touched a shock of awareness ran up his arm, and he had to force himself to let go of her hand before his coachman noticed his peculiarity.

Evie walked out onto a grassy field that gave an unimpeded view of the grand Castle and school for boys. "This is a good a place as any to set up for lunch."

Finn joined her, crouching down to sit with her in the grass. The ground was warm, if not a little damp. He'd not had a picnic like this since he was a child, and his nanny had taken him. "We're only a few hours from London from here. We shall break overnight at my London home before setting off for Scotland in a day or so. If we make good time, we may catch up with your sister before she ruins herself any further."

Not that he was going to save her now. Miss Lucy had made her choice and it was not him. She would live or die by her own sword. But he would ensure that Mr. Brown married the silly chit and by doing so, eliminating his association with Miss Lucy. He would not allow anyone of the gossiping *ton* to use his family as fodder for their amusement ever again. He'd endured such an existence when his father was alive. He would not do so again.

Evie sighed, and he glanced at her quickly, wondering what that sweet sound meant and hating the fact that his body reacted to it without warning or sense. "Why are you sighing and not saying anything, Evie? Is there something wrong with my plan?"

She opened the picnic basket that she had carried from the carriage, taking out two bread rolls and handing him one. "I'm curious as to why you would continue to chase Lucy when she's run off with another man. As a duke, I would think your choice is endless, and you may marry whomever you choose."

If only it were that simple. "Miss Lucy is from my home county and is young, and I thought unattached. She is from a good family and would have suited me very well." He paused. "However, I have given some thought to what you've said these past two days, about Lucy and her actions, and I no longer see a future between us. My travels north are now to ensure she marries, and neither mine or your family suffer the consequences socially of her choice."

"When it comes to matters of the heart, do you know that you speak with very little emotion? You sound as though you did not care for Lucy at all, or minded that she had run off with another man."

"I'm not a man of fanciful emotions or words," he stated, hating the fact that he was termed as someone without feeling.

She bit into a piece of ham, and his attention snapped to her mouth. Dear Lord, she chewed with the utmost sweetness.

"My father is a true gentleman, but we're not nobility. We're not rich nor are we part of the *beau monde*, and so I find it strange your courtship of my sister. Out of nowhere and without warning, I received a letter from Lucy that she was engaged and with you. A duke."

Evie was far more intelligent than he initially thought, and if he didn't watch his answers, he had no doubt she'd find out that he'd only offered for Lucy because he'd had no other choice. Why would he speak with emotion when he had none when it came to Lucy?

He was a bastard, and he should have fought his father's will instead of allowing his absurd clause to run his life.

"It is as you already know. I had business with your father and met Miss Lucy. She was a pleasant and jovial type of woman, and I thought she would suit as my bride." The lie tasted sour on his tongue.

He met Evie's steely, rich-brown eyes, and he had the overwhelming feeling that she could read his lie as if he'd written the word across his forehead. One eyebrow arched and he fought not to fidget where he sat. "Lucy has chosen another. Are you so set on your original course?"

"I cannot marry your sister now. Not after what she's done," he admitted. "I will not be part of such a scandal— a nefarious start to one's married life. But as a gentleman, I shall ensure she is married and limit the scandal on you and your family. Women who run away with their lovers always impact those who are left behind."

"I suppose London will have a juicy time with what Lucy has done, and I shall be talked about until the next scandalous thing occurs and takes their interest elsewhere." Her dejected tone did something odd to him inside, and he threw a piece of bread into his mouth less he be tempted to pull her into his arms and soothe her hurt.

The idea of Evie being talked about, taunted, and given the cut direct wasn't something he ever wished to see. For one, she did not deserve it and two, he had been right where Evie now sat. His father was forever causing scandals that were talked about for months. His friends at Eton would ask him of the stories, taunt and laugh at him. He'd not let that happen to her.

He poured them both a glass of red wine, handing one to Evie, determined to remove the dejected, sad expression that had befallen her features.

"What about you, Evie? You live in London and circulate in the same society as I do. I would have thought that a woman as attractive and intelligent as yourself would have been married by now." Finn swallowed a robust sip of wine. Today he seemed determined to bury himself in inappropriate compliments.

Her cheeks pinkened, and Finn had to admit that sometimes saying things that were not the way of a gentleman, or what he should talk to an unmarried woman about was worth it. Certainly, if he made her blush and made her porcelain skin turn a pretty shade of pink.

"No, there is not," she said, refusing to look at him. "I live in London with Molly and have not walked the same path as some of our friends have. My age doesn't make me the most sought-after woman at a ball, not that it ever made much difference when I was younger. As you know my family is not titled or rich. We're known more in Bath than in London, and I suppose I was found lacking."

"You are not lacking in any way," he said, cringing at his use of more inappropriate words. Soon he'd be as infamous as his father. He studied her a moment, watched as she chewed her sandwich of bread and ham. She tempted him. In fact, he wanted to do wicked and delightful things with her.

Since his father's death, he'd lived mostly in Wiltshire, looking after his estates and business dealings. Seeing Evie again, spending time with her, more time than he'd spent with Miss Lucy, all that occupied his mind since leaving Marlborough was what the woman before him would look like under him in his bed. Her long, chocolate locks spread about his pillow. Her sweet moans whispered against his ear as he brought her to climax.

"I'm sorry that we did not get to know each other well in London. We have mutual friends, have been to numerous balls and parties together and yet we have never spoken as honest and open as we have these past two days. I'm sorry for that." And he was. Never had he said anything more true. If he was to change his plan and court Evie to suit the clause in his father's will, more conversations such as these were what they needed. Evie required to like him in return and trust him.

A small smile played about her mouth, and he wanted to close the space between them and kiss her. To see if her lips were as soft as he imagined. It had been all he'd imagined last evening when he'd pulled her into his bed and hoisted her up against his chest. Her father would have him horsewhipped should he ever find out what he'd done, but he could not help himself. He'd wanted her in his arms for a night and so he'd pushed aside his dislike of scandal and had indulged himself.

Still, the thought of doing it again made him grin back at her. He'd suffer the wrath of anyone so long as he got to hold her again.

"I'm sorry too," she said, watching him. "Now tell me more about your estate. I've never been to Stoneheim Palace, but I hear it is lovely."

"My great grandfather built it and made a study of Blenheim Palace, hence the closeness of the name and design of the home. In fact, they're almost a mirror pair." They spoke for some time about each of their homes, and the local country near Marlborough and for the first time in his life, Finn did not feel as if he were putting on a mask or airs but was being merely himself. It was a heady feeling indeed and one he could get used to.

CHAPTER 9

They did not make London as planned after one of the carriage wheels lost a supporting bolt and threatened to fall off. Their journey into Salt Hill was slow, and it wasn't until the sun was low in the western sky that they arrived at the busy Windmill Inn. It was a setback that they did not need, not if they needed to ensure Lucy was indeed married and not just living in sin with Mr. Brown. Tomorrow they would push for London and travel on from there.

Even though the inn was busier than their accommodations of the night before, they were able to get separate rooms. The private dining room, unfortunately, was occupied, and so they had to break their fast in their accommodations.

Evie bade the duke goodnight just as the innkeeper's wife brought up their dinners of roast beef and vegetables along with red wine for her and ale for the duke, as his request.

The duke's room was across the hall from hers, and as the innkeeper's wife bustled about in Evie's room, setting her table for dining, nerves fluttered in Evie's stomach as she stood across from the duke about to bid him a good evening.

Something had changed between them today. Her body no longer felt itself, certainly not when Finn looked at her as he was right now, heavy-lidded and a slither of contemplation in his blue orbs. She shouldn't want him. He was still her sister's betrothed, sort of, she supposed. Even though he did state that he would not marry Lucy any longer and Lucy had said herself, she did not want the duke.

There was nothing, therefore, wrong with Evie finding him attractive, wondering what if... If he were willing.

"Do you think the carriage will be repaired in time for departure early tomorrow morning?" she asked, stepping aside as the innkeeper's wife went into the duke's room to prepare his table for dining.

"I should think so. There is a carriage maker here in Salt Hill, and he has promised to have it fixed for us posthaste. We will make London tomorrow as planned."

Evie thanked the innkeeper's wife as she bade them good night. For a moment, Evie stared at the duke, her body a riot of emotions, of wants and needs. She took a calming breath, pushing down the urge to throw herself at him and see where it would lead. If anywhere. "Well, thank you for the lovely day. I shall see you in the morning."

"Goodnight, Evie. Sleep well."

"Goodnight," she said, closing her door before the duke went back into his room.

Evie bathed and dressed for bed, climbing under the covers and wishing she were home where she could sneak down to the library and choose a book to read. Or merely huddle before her fire in her comfortable room and think about anything but the man who occupied the room across the hall from her.

What was wrong with her that he occupied so much of her mind? He never had before. They had barely spoken in London, there should be no reason at all that he did so now, but he did. He was a duke. She was an improvised spinster. They could not be more opposite.

And yet, he made her heart thump loud in her chest and her skin to prickle with awareness. She'd never had that with anyone before in her life, and she was loathe to lose it.

But maybe she didn't have to. If her sister was married and the duke looked for another to be his wife, maybe that another could be her.

The thought thrilled and scared her equally.

Evie sighed, rolling to her side and staring over to her window. She'd forgotten to close the curtains, and the moonlit night bathed a small square of the room's floor in light.

The bellow of a man out in the corridor, followed by running footsteps on the wooden floorboard planks, pulled her from her thoughts. Evie gasped, sitting up.

Had she locked her door? A female voice joined that of a man's, and she sat still, listening to the altercation. The man's voice shouted over that of the woman's, something about her sleeping with the baker and how he was going to kill the bastard by choking him with his own bread.

A light knock on her door made her start, and getting out of bed, Evie searched her room, spotting the chamber pot behind a privacy screen. She picked it up, holding it at her side as she padded over to the door. "Who is it?" she asked, hoping her voice sounded more confident than she felt.

"It's me. Finn. Let me in."

The fear of the couple arguing left her in an instant, and another fear flowed through her. What did the duke want? What did she want to do if she were to have him to herself another night? Alone.

She reached for the handle, happy to find she had locked the door after all. Opening it a fraction, she took in the duke in all his glory. He wore only his shirt that was gaping at his neck. His hair was askew as if he too had just been pulled from sleep. Thankfully he wore breeches, and yet she could not stop her inspection of him like a person starved of sustenance. Her eyes took in his bare feet and she bit back a grin. He looked like he'd jumped from his bed to her door and it did odd, delicious things to her insides. "What is it, Your Grace?"

"Let me in, Miss Milton. There seems to be a domestic quarrel going on, and I need to ensure you remain safe."

Evie glanced down the hall and spotted the couple arguing, the husband or lover, or whoever he was, paced that end of the corridor, his hands gesturing while the woman tried to appease him.

She stepped back, opening the door wide, and the duke stepped inside. He closed and locked the door, leaning on it a moment. "I thought tonight would be better for you, but this inn seems to have people who like to argue with no regard or care to others who are staying within its walls. I do apologize, Evie."

Evie sighed, walking over to her bed and sitting on its end. "I'm not bothered by it, truly." Evie took in his state of undress, his shirt that gaped at the front, teasing her with glimpses of his muscular chest. Warmth thrummed between her thighs and she crossed her legs.

His gaze burned into her, his attention traveling over her like a tempting caress. Evie's breathing fastened, and she bit her lip, wishing her thoughts to be a reality. She was turning as scandalous as her sister.

He sat beside her. The bed dipped a little, and she fell into him. He shot a glance at her as if she'd startled him.

"I, ah, I just wanted to ensure you were safe," he said after a time, his voice a deep, husky rumble.

"I am perfectly well. Their argument did not wake me, however. I was already awake," she said, needing to stop talking now before she started blabbering nonsense. "I think she had an affair."

"Yes." He glanced at her, and the breath in her lungs seized. He was so very handsome, with his beautiful, blue orbs and chiseled jaw. How was this man not already someone's husband? Someone's lover? Although, she supposed he was already someone's lover. What duke didn't have a bevy of women chasing after his coattails.

For all the inner strength of self she possessed, nothing could tear her eyes from his. She could lose herself with this man. There was something about him that drew her in, captured her attention and made her want to stay.

"It seems to have quietened outside. You should probably leave," she whispered. Why, however, she could not fathom since they were alone.

"Yes," he whispered, not moving.

Nor did she want him to. She wanted him to kiss her. A need tore through her and Evie stood, facing him. He stared up at her, the longing in his eyes a reflection of hers she was certain.

"I'm going to kiss you, Finn." Evie swallowed her fear,

having never been so forward or demanding in her life. She wanted her first kiss to be with this man. This honorable, sweet duke who was chasing after her sister simply to ensure the scandal was not too great.

Evie shoved all thoughts of Lucy aside. Her sister had made her choice. She was in love with another man and was probably already married. Had asked Evie to ruin her understanding with the duke. There was nothing wrong with her stealing her first kiss.

She leaned down, closing the space between them and their lips touched. The last, flittering thought she had was that indeed his lips were as soft as she suspected.

~

*F*inn did not feel like himself. His body seized with need, with a desire to ravish the woman kissing him with such sweetness that his heart ached.

Without thought, he reached up, clasping her face. He deepened the kiss, thrusting his tongue against hers. She didn't start or seize in fear at his action. No, she did none of those things. Instead, she kissed him with the same frenzied need. Wrapped her arms about his neck and pushed herself against his chest.

Her shift was no barrier and the contours of her body, her breasts... Good God, luscious, heavy breasts teased his chest. Her long, thin legs that stood between his made his body ache. Fuck, he wanted her. Wanted her as he'd never wanted anyone in his life.

Their kiss deepened, turned incendiary, and she pushed against him, tumbling them back onto the bed. She came over him, their kiss never breaking, and hunger roared through him like a fever.

He was ravenous for her. Wanted her so much that had he been thinking rationally, it would scare him, but logical thought was a long way off at present, and so he let himself go. To simply enjoy her and her sweet mouth.

Finn rolled her onto her back, coming over her to settle between her legs. His cock rigid, his balls tight. He reached down, lifting one of her legs against his hip and pushed against her hot cunny.

It would be so easy to lean back, rip his front falls open, and thrust into her wet, welcoming heat. She undulated against his manhood, and he groaned, mimicking her and eliciting a delicious gasp from her sweet lips.

A loud crash sounded outside, and they started, the kiss ended. Like a bucket of cold water washing over them, Finn took stock of the position he was in and with whom. What was he doing? He had yet to decide if Evie was even a contender as his wife. He had planned on talking to his family doctor about Evie's chances of giving him children at her age. And here he was, hard as stone, poised to rip his breeches down and take her anyway.

This was not right, and not only for that reason. Two days ago, he'd been poised to marry her sister. He could not touch Evie until he was certain Lucy was married to Mr. Brown. What he would do after that, who he would marry, he had yet to decide.

Finn gazed down at Evie, her cheeks flushed red with exertion, her lips full and a little bruised from his kiss. She looked ripe enough to eat, and the thought of losing himself in her was a temptation hard to deny, but he had to.

"I must go. I'm sorry," he managed, crawling off her and ignoring the sight of her lying pliant and ready for a lover—his loving.

He adjusted his clothing, before opening the door and watching as the drunken man stumbled wobbly down the hallway before disappearing into a room. "Goodnight, Evie," he said, not looking back. To do so would mean one thing. That he would not leave, and that was not an option.

Not now, at least.

CHAPTER 10

*E*vie bathed and dressed early after sleep eluded her. Last night when the duke had come into her room, she'd seemed to have lost all control of self. Her body had burned with a need that she'd never experienced before. It ached for his touch, for his kiss, for things that no unmarried woman should ache for. She'd wanted nothing more than to rip down his breeches, take him in hand and make him hers.

She'd wanted to be filled and inflamed, wanted more of his delectable, deep kisses that left her head spinning. What her sister Lucy did not see in the duke, she could not fathom. He was a duke to start, above whom either of them ever thought to marry. He was kind and loyal; his helping of their family to ensure Lucy was married before moving on with his life was proof of that.

Even so, after last night, Evie knew for the first time in her life what it felt like when one wanted something they could not have. She didn't just want to divert the duke away from marrying Lucy as her sister had asked. Oh no, now she wanted him for herself.

But how to make a duke see her more than a spinster —a woman who was far beneath him in rank and riches.

Evie packed up her things, placing them in her small valise and left the room, heading downstairs. The carriage was hitched and waiting at the inn yard by the time she arrived. The wheel once again adequately attached to the carriage with the correct amount of bolts. Evie placed her small bag inside the vehicle, wanting to go for a short walk before they left.

The duke was nowhere to be seen, and so Evie found the carriage driver. "Dickens, I'm just going to go for a short walk down high street. I shall not be more than a few minutes."

The carriage driver tipped his hat. "Right ye are, Miss Milton. I shall inform His Grace when I see him."

"Thank you," Evie said. She left the bustling inn and started walking down the main town's thoroughfare. There were a few stores, a bakery, numerous houses and other inns that looked as busy as the Windmill. Few people were out at this early hour, and she took her time, enjoying the solitude and exercise that she would not get again for several hours.

Today's journey to London should not take as long as yesterday, and with any success, they would not have any issues with the carriage that could hold them up. In London, the duke had stated he would inquire as to whether Lucy and Mr. Brown had traveled through or stopped. A small part of Evie hoped they had continued on to Scotland. They would be near impossible to find in London, and if they were still on the road, Evie could spend more time with the duke.

Alone.

After last night, the crisp, fresh country air had helped clear Evie's thoughts. Her sister did not want the duke, so if she were to pursue him, make him see her more than his scandalous ex-betrothed sister, there was nothing wrong with that. It was not against the law.

The kiss they shared told her more than anything they would suit. His kiss had lit a light within her, a light she could not see ever going out. It was not a sweet, chaste kiss on the cheek or lips, but a total ravishment, one that left her mouth tingling, her body longing long after he'd left her room.

She wanted more, and Evie was anything if not resourceful when she wanted something.

"Miss Milton, is that you? Miss Milton!"

Evie glanced across the street and stilled at the sight of Miss Emma Malcolm, an heiress who lived in the same square as she did in London and newly betrothed to Earl Mcfarlane. The young woman was sweet of nature, but a terrible gossiper. Evie looked back toward the inn, and inwardly sighed at not being able to make her escape before being besieged.

"Miss Malcolm, how very nice to see you here. What brings you to Salt Hill?"

The young woman chuckled, coming to stand before her on the street, her maid a little way behind. "Oh, my father's estate is but a mile from here. We've been home preparing for my marriage to the earl but will be returning to London tomorrow, in fact. What brings you to Salt Hill?"

Evie furiously thought of what to say. She supposed she could tell the truth. That her sister had run off with a farmer after agreeing to marry a duke, and now she and that said duke were chasing after her. "I too, am returning to London. Today in fact. I have been home visiting family in Wiltshire."

"How lovely for you. Only yesterday I ran into your sister, I believe. You introduced me to her last Season when she came up to London for several weeks if you remember." Miss Malcolm frowned, pursing her lips. "However, she did not have a maid, and she was traveling with a man who did not seem her equal if you do not mind my saying. He was not dressed as smart as Miss Lucy was, and seemed distracted, almost as if he was expecting someone to come up behind him or something."

Evie fought not to clasp Miss Malcolm's arms and shake more information from her. She'd seen Lucy, and only yesterday! Which would mean they were likely in London today. Perhaps they would halt their travels north a day or so and give Evie and the duke time in catching up to them.

"Ah, yes, Lucy was traveling ahead of me. I shall meet up with her in town tomorrow."

"Your cousin said as much," Miss Malcolm said.

"My cousin?" Evie queried.

"Well yes." Miss Malcolm chuckled, but even Evie could hear the thread of nervousness that entered her tone. "The gentleman with Miss Lucy. He introduced himself as your cousin. A farmer, which I suppose thinking about it, would explain why he looked so poorly dressed."

Miss Malcolm's pretty face drained of color. "I do apologize, Miss Milton. I did not mean to be so rude."

Evie waved her interpretation of Mr. Brown aside, her mind whirring with news of Lucy. She had to return to the inn and tell the duke. This was good news. "I must leave you now, Miss Malcolm, but I wish you safe travels to

London tomorrow and do wish you very happy with your upcoming nuptials."

The young woman beamed, pleasure written across her features. "Thank you, Miss Milton. I'll be sure to send you an invitation."

Evie dipped into a curtsy. "It will be a pleasure to attend. Good day to you." Evie waved goodbye and started back toward the inn at a clipped pace. Of all the towns to run into someone from London, and not just anyone, but a dedicated gossiper was beyond unlucky. And Lucy too. But the news on Lucy was just what Evie needed to hear. At least they had traveled the same way, and they were only a day behind her. A niggling concern of Evie's had been that Lucy and Mr. Brown had gone to Bath and traveled north from there. The journey was much quicker and smoother on the great north road, but there had been no hint as to which way they would go.

She rounded into the inn-yard, and her steps faltered at the sight of the duke, pacing behind the carriage, his great-coat flying behind him like a cape. Pleasure replaced all thoughts of her sister a moment, and she just enjoyed the sight of the duke, his tall athleticism on full display for any who were watching him.

"Where did you go?" the duke demanded, coming to a stop and pinning her with his gaze. "I thought something terrible had befallen you."

Evie came to stand before him, tipping up her chin to meet his gaze. "I went for a walk, and I have news of Lucy."

"You do?" All annoyance at her stroll disappeared, and he pulled her over to the carriage, helping her inside. The duke joined her, seating himself across from her.

"What are you doing?"

"I'm traveling in the carriage. I do not feel like riding today."

"What about your horse?" she asked, looking out the window as their coachman walked the duke's horse past the carriage window.

"He's being tied to the back of the carriage. He'll be fine there."

Evie wasn't sure what she thought about the duke being in such close confines to her once again, especially after last evening. The carriage was opulent and roomy, but he was overbearing, took up too much room of the space.

The trip to London would be lengthy indeed…

He studied her a moment, and she fought not to fidget with the sleeve of her dress. "Tell me of this news of Miss Lucy. How is it that you found out this information?"

"I wanted to go for a walk, as I said. I knew we were going to have a lengthy carriage ride today, and I wanted to exercise before we departed. I ran into Miss Malcolm. You may have heard she's recently engaged to the Earl Mcfarlane."

He nodded, turning to stare out the carriage window just as the equipage dipped as the coachman climbed up onto the box. The duke knocked on the roof, and the carriage lurched forward. "I had not heard that news, no, but tell me more of your sister. She was here in Salt Hill. Recently I presume."

"Only yesterday. Miss Malcolm ran into her and Mr. Brown, so at least we know that they are together. They were traveling to London and are only a day ahead of us."

The duke rubbed his jaw in thought. "With any luck, they will halt their progress in town before traveling north. We may not have to go all the way to Gretna, after all, to ensure your sister marries this Mr. Brown."

"That was my hope too." Evie didn't feel like traveling all the way to Gretna, not any longer at least. Days on end in a carriage and nights at inns where not all of them were guaranteed to be comfortable nor clean. It was not ideal. "What is the plan once we arrive in London?" she asked.

"We shall return to my townhouse. I will send out my man of business to try and locate Miss Lucy and Mr. Brown. See if they are still in town or have traveled north."

"I can return to my home in London if that suits. If we're to be in London a day or so, I should probably not be staying under your roof." Not that Evie didn't want to spend more time with Finn, she did, desperately so, but it wasn't right, and she didn't need to bring any more scandal onto her family. Her sister had done enough of that already.

"About last evening, Evie."

Evie held up her hand, not wanting him to profess how much he regretted their kiss or to chastise her over insti-gating her lack of decorum. She didn't want to hear how it was wrong and why it would not happen again. "There is nothing to discuss."

"I would disagree with that summarization."

Evie swallowed the nerves that fluttered in her stomach at the near mention of them kissing. She met his gaze, resigned to hear him out. "Very well, you want to discuss our kiss?"

His attention dipped to her lips, and nerves skittered across her skin. The air seemed to evaporate in the carriage, expectation thrumming through her.

He cleared his throat. "Yes, the kiss. I wanted you to know that I hold no ill will toward you over your conduct. I've thought about it and have concluded that you were upset over the argument outside our rooms and required comforting."

Evie's lips twitched, and she couldn't hold back a chuckle at his reasoning. "That wasn't why I kissed you, Finn." The kiss had a lot more to do with her wanting him than it did about anything else.

He stared at her, his face an unreadable mask. "Why did you kiss me then?"

"I kissed you because I wanted to kiss you. Not because I was scared for my safety. I like you and the way that you were looking at me last night," Evie said, shrugging. "I thought that you might like to kiss me too."

A muscle in his jaw clenched, and he turned to look out the window. It was not the response that she wanted to see, but then she'd never thrown herself at a duke before, there was no telling how these aristocratic men would react. "Honor dictates that I ensure Miss Lucy is married before anything can happen with anyone else. I know that my understanding with your sister was at an end the moment she ran off with Mr. Brown, but still, I should not have kissed you. It was wrong, and I apologize."

Evie pushed away the stab of pain his words caused and settled back into the plush, leather seat. "Had you ever kissed Lucy, Your Grace?" she asked, reverting to titles since his kiss with her was wrong. The fiend. It had not been wrong. It had been wonderful, and if he only could admit that, there may be hope for them after all.

"Of course not." His words came out a little scandalized and she wondered why. Why would kissing his betrothed seem so undone. "I have not known Miss Lucy for very long and did not feel she was open to such affections," he said, rubbing a hand over his jaw.

Evie watched his hand slide against his face, marred by

only the slightest shadow of impending stubble. The memory of those lips upon hers, her skin abraded by his ardent kiss, bombarded her, and she wiggled on her seat. Perhaps, at her advanced age of seven and twenty, she had long run out of patience and wanted more. Wanted a husband who could kiss her, love her as much and as often, as she wanted.

"I suppose I understand now why Miss Lucy was not interested in kissing me. I was not her choice."

"I am sorry my sister has done this to you, but I cannot be sorry for her choice. Had you married Lucy, she would not have been happy, and your marriage would have suffered for it. I think any couple who marry must respect and like each other and have a mutual desire if they're to endure a lifetime. I know that is what I want when I marry. I want to desire my husband, to want to be near him as much and as often as I'd like."

The muscles on his jaw tightened, and his eyes heated as they watched her. Her words held more meaning than face value. Scandalous talk that the duke did not like, but Evie could not help it. He maddened her no end. "We have many hours ahead of us in this equipage. Did you bring your book today, Evie?"

"I did not, no," she replied. Now that they were alone, on the road to London, all she could think of doing was kissing him again. Of having his hands on her, his body pushing against hers in the most inappropriate fashion. His disapproval of the action only made her want to do it more. "A game of cards perhaps. Did you bring a pack, Your Grace?"

He cringed. "I did not, no," he said, mimicking her words.

"Well then," Evie said, grinning across the space at

him. "You'll just have to kiss me again to pass the time. That will be just as diverting."

CHAPTER 11

inn cleared his throat, wondering if he'd just heard correctly. Had Evie told him to kiss her again after he'd just told her they could not do such things? She was a temptation he could not deny, no matter how many times he told her or himself that he should leave her alone. A small part of him felt that if he dallied with her, it was wrong. He was still to decide if he would pursue her as his future bride, but after last evening the idea of having Evie in his bed for the rest of his life was an idea that made sense to him. Even now, he wanted to wrench her onto his lap and take that sweet mouth with his. Touch her, lose himself in her willing heat.

Finn inwardly groaned. He'd turned into his father—a man with no self-control.

Her wicked, teasing grin that beckoned across from him was not helping him in the slightest, and the minx damn well knew it. He'd hardly slept last evening, having tossed and turned all night. For a time, he'd debated taking himself in hand and releasing his aroused state.

There was something about Evie that drew him in,

made him question everything that he thought he'd wanted. A bride some years younger than himself, from a wealthy, noble family. Evie was none of those things, and yet still, it was she that made the blood in his veins pump at a heady beat.

God damn it, he needed to get a grip on himself. He shifted on his seat, his cock coming to attention when her pink tongue slipped out and wet her bottom lip. "Tell me you did not just ask me to kiss you again," he said in the sternest voice he could manage. "Have you not been listening as to why we cannot kiss again?"

"I have been listening," she said, no shame in her voice. "I'm not engaged, and after my sister's decision two days ago, neither are you. We're not doing anything wrong if we were to pass the time in such a delightful way. No one need ever know, so it is not scandalous to act on our desires."

Delightful?

He found her kisses just so as well. "Whether kissing was delightful or not, we should refrain from doing so again. For a time, at least."

Finn stilled when Evie leaned forward, and the sight of her breasts in her traveling gown caught his attention. She was dressed today in a dark-navy gown and cream pelisse, and she was utter perfection.

He forced himself back into the squabs, away from her delectable, tempting self. "You should not throw yourself at gentlemen like you do. You may find one day a gentleman will take you up on your teasing and ask for more than you're willing to give."

"If that happens, then he is no gentleman. And I do not throw myself at anyone. Indeed, my friends can attest to the validity of my statement. That is, until now, with you. Why will you not kiss me again? Did you not enjoy yourself?"

Enjoy himself? He'd reveled in the delight of having her in his arms. Of losing himself in her kiss, her little whimpers, and sighs. "It was adequate."

"Adequate? Oh no, we cannot have that."

Before Finn knew what was happening, Evie was beside him on the seat, staring up at him, a wicked, teasing grin on her pretty visage. She was a handsome woman, with her long, dark chocolate locks and rose-colored lips. It made him wonder why she'd never been swooped off her feet and carried to the altar. How was it that she had not become someone's wife a long time ago?

"Why are you not married, Evie?"

"Me?" she asked, taken aback at his question. She sat back a little, and Finn breathed deep once more. Having her so near did odd things to his mind, made it cloudy and thick and not at all like he usually was, thorough and clear of thought.

"Yes, you. You're a handsome woman, your father is a gentleman, and your friends are highly placed in society. Why is it that you have never married?"

"You're trying to distract me from kissing you again, are you not, Your Grace?"

He didn't like being back to titles, but perhaps it was necessary. They should not be kissing and fondling each other. Not yet, at least.

"Have you never been courted?" he asked, refusing to answer her question.

She leaned back in the squabs and glanced out the window a moment before she said, "I was sent away to school in France. I met my friends at Madame Dufour's Refining School for Girls, before they had married into the *ton*. I suppose over the many years of watching them all be courted and then married, I have missed my chance at finding love.

"Before Willow inherited Viscountess Vance's fortune, I had to return to my father's small estate at the end of each Season. Some years my family could not afford to send me to London to join my friends in the Season, and so I spent that time away from society and opportunities to meet new people. Time went by, and now I am seven and twenty. An old maid to some."

"I feel we have missed an opportunity with us both being in Wiltshire and having never met there." He'd been so distracted with trying to distance himself from his father, keeping the estate running while his sire had sown his seed all over London, creating scandals wherever he went, that he had not looked up to see who was around him. Even in London he'd known of Evie, had danced with her, and still, he'd walked away from her without a backward glance. A foolish mistake. "I have not spent much time in London these past years. And then the death of my father a year ago has kept me busy."

"I did hear that he passed away. I'm very sorry for your loss."

"Don't be," he said automatically. "He never cared for his family, only his whores. Even now beyond the grave, he is trying to rule my life."

"How so?" she asked, glancing at him curiously.

Finn started, realizing that he'd said too much. An easy feat when talking to Miss Milton. When she was not trying to kiss him, she was a very good listener and spoke common sense, no silly debutante who giggled and blushed every time one spoke. He liked her maturity. It suited him and his character better than Miss Lucy ever had. Evie's younger sister had been a little bit of giggler and smiled a little too often for his liking. Not that he didn't want a wife who smiled, but he would've preferred one who did not grin like a lunatic at everyone she came in contact with.

"I only meant," he continued, "that his reputation has tarnished my own. No matter what you may have heard about me, Evie, I am nothing like my father. Not in any way other than the title that I inherited from him."

She reached out and clutched his arm, squeezing it a little before letting him go. "You're an honorable man, Finn. No matter what, nothing can change my opinion of you." The moment her hand slipped from his arm, he missed her touch. He liked Evie touching him, and little else occupied his mind of late. He was not like his father, he repeated in his mind. Kissing an unmarried woman did not make him debauched like his sire.

"Thank you," he said, her words meaning more than any he'd heard from anyone before.

The carriage turned and, glancing out the window, Finn took in the less-pretty landscape of scrubby acreage that was marred by gravel pits. "We'll luncheon at The Magpies at Uxbridge. The fare is satisfactory there."

"I stopped there on my way home. Their beef pie is tasty indeed," Evie said, leaning over him to look out the window even though she had one on her side. "Perhaps we can spend our time occupied in other ways after all, Finn. You may not have to kiss me again if we're to keep up such lively conversation such as the one we just had."

Finn chuckled, yet inwardly he could not stop thinking about every which way he could instigate another kiss with the delectable Evie. Lively conversation be damned.

~

*E*vie woke with a start several hours later after a hearty lunch at Uxbridge, as promised. The carriage rolled to an abrupt halt. She sat up, rubbing her neck and realized that she'd been sleeping on Finn. She threw him a small smile and glanced out the window. This was not her house, and from the look of the massive Georgian mansion they'd pulled up before, this was most definitely the duke's.

As promised, the duke had not tried to kiss her again on their journey into town. Instead, he had purchased a pack of cards from the inn where they had broken their fast, and they had played several games of *vingt-et-un* before she'd begged for a reprieve to simply relax and enjoy her last few hours with the duke.

It was only a matter of time before she'd grown tired from the rocking of the carriage and had fallen asleep. That she'd woken up with her head in the duke's lap was not what she'd imagined when she'd closed her eyes.

Evie sat up, the duke stilling as she came to sit up next to him. She glanced at him and saw that he too looked like he'd just woken up from slumber. "I do apologize, Finn. I did not mean to make use of your lap in such a way."

He adjusted his seat, rubbing a hand over his jaw as he tried to take in his surroundings. "Do not trouble yourself, Miss Milton. No one shall ever know that we've slept together."

Heat rushed up her neck to settle on her cheeks. She glanced at him quickly and read the horror that his words wrecked on his visage.

"I do apologize, Evie. My words came out wrong. I merely meant to say that our napping in the carriage was perfectly normal and not in any way untoward. We're fully clothed, are we not?"

Evie glanced down at her gown just to make sure she was indeed fully clothed. "We're stopping here for the night?" she asked, wanting to change the subject. How could she have fallen asleep with her head in the duke's lap? Her mother would suffer apoplexy if she knew. As for her father, he would demand a wedding. "I thought you were taking me to my home with Molly."

"We are," he said, seemingly thankful for her change of subject. "It is very late, and I did not want to throw your household into an uproar at your return. My staff is expecting us, and they will have a room ready for you. No one will ever know you stayed here. It is only for one night. I shall return you to your home tomorrow should we not need to travel north after your sister."

Evie was too tired to argue with his plan and simply took his hand, thankful for his support as she stepped out of the carriage for the first time in as many hours. Her back ached, and she leaned back, trying to loosen her tight, sore muscles. "May I have a bath brought to my room, Your Grace. I am terribly sore and tired."

"Of course, I shall have one ordered at once."

"Thank you." They made their way indoors, and Evie couldn't help but be awed by the grandeur that met her. Marble-lined the walls, a spiraling oak staircase led upstairs and large, family portraits hung along the walls, all of the dukes of the past staring down and judging her for the commoner she was.

The butler bowed, taking the duke's greatcoat. "Your rooms are ready, Your Grace, and we have dinner waiting for you whenever you're ready to eat."

"Thank you, George," Finn said, he too rolling his

shoulders. "A tray in our rooms will do very well, and can you have a bath brought up for Miss Milton?"

The butler bowed once more. "Of course." He gestured toward the staircase. "Would you like me to escort you to your room, Miss Milton?"

Evie glanced at the duke, and he smiled in agreement. "Goodnight, Miss Milton."

"Goodnight, Your Grace." Evie went with the servant up the long flight of stairs before walking down a well-lit passageway that too was lined with family portraits and an abundance of hothouse flowers.

She'd seen similar opulence in Ava's, Willow's and Hallie's homes, and yet to see the man whom she had been kissing the past two days was as fortunate as her friends filled her with unease. Of course, she'd always known he was a duke, but she'd never seen just how wealthy he was. It made his betrothal to Lucy, and her dreams of having him for herself seem feeble, if not impossible. Made her feel inferior and unworthy. There were so many rich noble-women who would suit him better, who had been raised to marry such a man. She was not one of them.

The butler opened the door to her room for the night, and Evie was unable to stop the gasp of delight at seeing her chamber. The walls were painted a light, bright cream, but the bedding was a rich green, the dark, wooden furniture giving the room a masculine feel, but so very beautiful. Evie stepped across the threshold, going to the bed to run her hand along the silk cover.

Just as promised, Evie broke her fast and then soaked in a bath that two footmen brought up for her. She sat before the fire, drying her hair when a light knock sounded on her door. Nerves fluttered in her stomach, and she pulled her dressing gown closed before opening it.

Evie cracked the door a little to find Finn standing before her. "Is there something wrong?" she asked, searching for words and unsure what to say now that they were alone once more and in his house. No one to interrupt them.

"I, ah…" he stammered, his attention moving over her shoulder to take in her room. "I hope you find your accommodations are to your liking."

Evie nodded, glancing back into the space, her bed like a beacon of temptation, more so now that the duke was standing before her. "It's lovely. I don't think I've ever had such a beautiful room before."

"You should always have beautiful things," he said, his voice low and gravelly.

Her heart twisted at his sweet words, and for a moment, she could not move. She wanted to lean up and kiss him, to take more of what she knew he could give her, but she did not. Her brazenness had seemed to have deserted her after today when he'd gone above and beyond in keeping his distance. Maybe he did not want to kiss her anymore, and she'd been fooling herself into thinking that the one kiss they had shared meant anything at all. To the duke, at least.

The thought left her depleted, and she stepped back into the room. A hand shot out and clasped her arm, pulling her back.

"Goodnight then, Evie," he whispered, closing the space between them, his lips but a feather width from hers. Her knees threatened to give way as he closed that small space between them and kissed her. She was sure he'd meant it to be a chaste kiss, merely a goodnight between friends, but it was not chaste in any way.

The moment his lips touched hers, he deepened the

kiss, his tongue twisting with hers and sending her wits to spiral. Evie reached up, clasping his shoulders to stop herself from falling to the ground at the pleasure of it. She'd wanted him to kiss her, wanted so much to be back in his arms, and for him to kiss her this time left a heady feeling spiraling through her blood. He stepped against her, walking her back until she came up against the wall beside her door. Pleasure and need shot through her, her body not her own, but his to have.

Evie had never been with a man before. Something told her this was the desire her friends had spoken about when they had discussed their marriages. How one look, a touch or small smile could send their wits spinning and make them follow their spouse to see where their interlude would lead.

"I shouldn't want you as much as I do," he said against her lips before kissing her again. The kiss was unlike any she'd ever known, not that she'd known any before, but chaste was not what was going on right now between them.

He kissed her as if he were starved of her touch. As if he wished to devour every ounce of her flesh. She shivered at the thought of him kissing her elsewhere, of his tongue that now tangled with hers, tasting her skin, her body, in the most private of places.

"Do not stop," she begged, kissing him with as much desire as she could. Still, she could not get enough of him. And then his hands slipped down her body, past her breasts to settle on her hips before skating behind and clasping her bottom. He wrenched her up against his body, undulating against her core. Evie moaned, liquid heat pooling between her legs.

"Finn," she gasped, clutching at him like a lifeline. Never had she felt as she did right now. As if she would wither and die if he did not continue what he had started. And he had started this. He had kissed her this time.

The sound of footsteps on the staircase sounded, and Finn pulled away, going to stand out in the hall just as the butler came toward them. "Your Grace, your steward is here, as you requested."

"Thank you, George. Please tell Mr. Cleavers I will be down directly."

"Of course, Your Grace," the servant said, leaving them as quickly as he arrived.

Finn sighed, turning back toward Evie. "I should go. I need to speak to my steward about your sister and Mr. Brown. See what he can find."

"Of course," Evie said, taking a calming breath and hoping he did not notice that her heart beat a thousand times too fast. "Let us hope they are in London, and we can find them."

"Yes." The duke stepped back into her room and kissed her yet again. Evie gasped, reveling in his touch, before he wrenched free, striding down the hallway to meet his steward. Evie closed the door and slumped against it when closed. A small smile slipped onto her lips. After those two kisses, it would seem the duke was not so unaffected as he'd claimed. Perhaps there was a chance for them, after all.

CHAPTER 12

*T*he following morning brought news that her sister and Mr. Brown were indeed in London and had not traveled north to Scotland. The report was both pleasing and worrying at the same time. Did Mr. Brown intend to marry Lucy at all, or was he simply enjoying his time with her away from the security of her family?

Evie sat at the breakfast table, the duke reading over the paper beside her, and she could not help but think that this is how a married couple may break their fast. The duke had told her of the news he'd found and was now reading the paper.

"We need to travel down to St. Giles and see if we can flush them out. Would you come with me?" he asked suddenly, looking at her for an answer.

Evie set her cup of tea down, unsure she'd heard him right. "You wish for me to come with you?"

"I do." He folded his paper, placing it to his side. "Which brings me to something else that I wanted to discuss with you. Regarding your accommodations while in London."

Evie frowned, having thought they had already discussed where she'd stay. "I thought I was returning to my normal place of residence in London."

He studied her a moment before he said, "I want you to stay here, Evie. With me. No one knows we're in London trying to chase down your sister to limit her ruination. If it becomes known that we are, that we are here and why, it will only make the situation worse for everyone. I have spoken to my staff and steward and notified them all that as far as they are concerned, we're both still in Wiltshire and will not be back in London for several weeks yet."

Evie took in his plan and could see sense in it. The thought of staying under the duke's roof, hiding themselves away from the world with only themselves for company. "Very well, but what if we are seen? My reputation will be ruined."

"It will not be. I will not let it." The determination in his tone soothed the small amount of trepidation at his plan.

"If you're sure. I will stay here with you." Evie pushed back from the table, starting for the door. "If we're traveling into St. Giles, I need to go change."

"What is wrong with your gown?" the duke asked, calling after her.

Evie paused at the threshold of the room, turning to face the duke. "You should change as well. If we want to blend into those who live in that seedy part of London, you had better take off those highly polished hessian boots and superfine coat. You'll be mugged before we take two steps from the carriage door.

~

*F*inn grinned at Evie as she disappeared out into the foyer. Warmth seeped into his bones at the knowledge she was going to stay in his home for some days. Just the two of them, nestled away from the *ton*, and only themselves for company.

At this point, he was becoming less and less troubled by Miss Lucy and Mr. Brown, finding them, or the scandal all of this would cause if people found out. He'd promised Evie's father he would help in ensuring his daughter was not ruined, but other than that, there was little between him and his ex-betrothed.

Finn pushed back his chair, starting for his room to change, as Evie suggested. Under an hour later, they were in the carriage and heading down toward St. Giles. The area where his steward had heard word that Miss Lucy was staying.

Evie sat beside him in the carriage, her lip clasped between her teeth as she glanced outside. The streets of Mayfair soon gave way to the more impoverished areas of town, showcasing the struggles that the poor faced every day.

"Do not worry, Evie. I have brought a flintlock, and I'm not incapable of looking after myself."

"But are you capable of looking after us both should we get in trouble?" She glanced back at him. "Did you bring any money? I cannot pass a child in need and not give them anything."

He nodded and tapped the pocket on his chest. The jacket he'd borrowed from one of his stable staff was surprisingly comfortable and befitted this expedition. "I do. You may give it all away if you wish."

She wrapped her arm about his, pulling herself close to his side. "I knew that you were a good man. A trait that you keep proving to me time and again." Her sweet face tipped up toward his and did odd things to his insides. Finn took the opportunity to lean down and take her lips.

His body roared with possession, and he took her mouth, sliding his tongue against hers. She tasted of tea and the honey that she'd put on her toast this morning. The idea of having this woman always occupied his mind as much as the idea of her in his bed, and it would not abate. Evie Milton suited him, was of similar character and sensible. She would make a good duchess and wife, even at seven and twenty.

Her hands clasped the lapels of his coat, pulling him closer, and he took the opportunity to touch her. Her dress was coarse wool, nothing like the clothes she usually wore. In fact, breaking the kiss, he took in her gown, frowning.

"What is it you have on? That cannot be comfortable," he said, taking in the coarse wool and ill-fitting cut.

"It's one of the scullery maid's gowns. I paid her to use it and she was more than happy to part with it then." She took in his own attire. "You're looking very handsome yourself. I think I like seeing you look so very rugged."

He chuckled, sitting back against the squabs but not before taking her hand and holding it in his lap. A simple, sweet gesture that felt as natural as kissing her did.

The carriage turned around a corner, and Finn gauged their location. "We should be there soon."

"Do you think we'll find Lucy today?" Evie looked up at him with expectation, and he wished he could tell her they would, but he wasn't sure. His steward had said that although there had been sightings of the couple, the exact location of their quarters was not yet known.

"We'll walk about the streets where I was told they had been seen. Maybe they will be out and about and we shall spot them." Finn had taken the precaution of having two burly stable men on the back of the carriage who would be with them, and his driver was not unarmed. He'd not usually take a woman into this part of town, but Evie was the only one of them who knew what Mr. Brown looked like. He himself had never met the fellow.

A little while later, the carriage pulled up on Newman street and Finn helped Evie alight. He took in their location and those who took note of their arrival. He pulled her close and started up the narrow, cobbled street, clothing hanging across the space above their heads and children running about, their feet bare.

Evie reached into his pocket, taking the few coins he'd brought and gave one to a little girl who held out her hand. "I hate seeing children with so little. Our government should do more to help the poor."

Finn couldn't agree more, and he often gave to charities and orphanages. The task of pulling the poor out of their substandard living needed more than one's duke's funds. It required everyone to partake in their rise.

They took in the people they passed, Evie looking up and down the alleyways they crossed. The area became dank and of worse conditions the longer they walked about. "I cannot believe Lucy would stay in such an area. Mr. Brown was a farmer. Surely he had some funds to pay for better lodgings than those this area offers."

"It would seem he did not." Finn hated telling Evie such truths, but for Lucy to be living in such conditions, away from her family and friends, there was a good chance that she had ruined herself beyond repair, and they may not be able to keep her actions private for long.

They turned up an alleyway, Evie handing out more coins to a group of children who all jumped and hooted at their windfall before running off. The lane opened up to a circular group of two-story houses. All of them were of wood construction, windows broken, and wood rotten and missing in some places. There was a decided odor of urine and human feces and Finn cringed.

Evie gasped, her body stilling beside him, and he glanced at her quickly, seeing her widened eyes and pale skin. "What is it?" he asked, taking her hand and shaking it a little when she did not answer.

"Someone threw something onto my dress from above." Her eyes filled with tears, and Finn glanced up, seeing a smirking, large woman leaning out the window.

"'Ave a good day, my lady," the woman said, tipping her chamber pot over the windowsill once again to ensure it was empty.

Finn glared at the lady before she disappeared inside. "Come, we'll return home. There is always tomorrow."

"I cannot get in your carriage with this muck on me, Finn. The smell will never come out."

"Never mind that. I'll buy a new carriage." He pulled her back to where they came, never seeing Lucy or Mr. Brown on their wanderings. It did not matter, they would be found soon enough, and then Finn would ensure the blaggard married the woman he stole from her home or he didn't know what he would do.

One thing he was certain was that he would not let Evie suffer the fate of her sister's actions. He would not allow an ounce of scandal to touch himself or Evie.

They arrived back at the mews of his townhouse, and Finn helped Evie return inside, ordering the house staff to bring up water for a bath. He fought not to cringe at the scent permeating off her clothing, which would have to be burned.

"I'm humiliated," she said beside him as he helped her up the stairs. Thankfully the urine had missed her hair and had merely hit her back first before running down the rear of her gown. "I'm so sorry, Finn. Your carriage may never smell the same again."

He chuckled, taking her arm and pulling it around his own. "You'll be clean soon, and the carriage is nothing. It wasn't your fault that it happened."

"Thank you, Finn."

Finn walked her to her door, opening it for her. "I'll send a maid up to help you undress and prepare for your bath. It will be up soon, and then you'll feel better."

"Since I'm a woman, standing before you and smelling of someone else's bodily fluid, you're very sweet to say so."

He tipped up her chin, leaning down and kissing her, not caring if any of his household staff saw them. "Enjoy your bath, Evie. I'll have lunch sent up to you on a tray if you wish."

"Thank you," she said, stepping into the room and gifting him one last look before closing the door. Finn took a calming breath, pushing away the thought of her stripping off her clothes and stepping into the hot, fragrant bathwater.

Naked.

He groaned, forcing his feet to his room to change. He could pursue her without impediment once Lucy was married and voiding his understanding with her once and for all. And then, *then*, he could pursue what was becoming a little bit of an obsession.

Evie.

CHAPTER 13

*E*vie stared a moment as the door closed, separating her and duke once more. It was becoming harder and harder to keep her distance from him, from asking him if what she was starting to suspect was between them was only on her side.

She did not think that was the case, but it was hard to tell what the duke was thinking most of the time unless those times were when he was kissing her, and then she knew what he was feeling.

A knock sounded, startling her, and she opened the door, a little disappointed to see footmen carrying a large hip bath and buckets, a maid behind them also with drying linens and a cake of soap. Evie stepped back, bidding them enter and watched as they set it up before the stoked fire, giving her inspecting glances now and then.

She supposed she deserved their inspection. She was, after all, an unmarried woman living under the same roof as their master. They probably thought she was his mistress, but the way she felt right at this moment, she did not feel very mistress-like. She felt like a cesspit.

The maid helped her undress, and Evie dismissed her, asking her to burn the gown immediately. Both Lucy and she were used to bathing on their own and not needing anyone to help. The water was fragrant and smelled of lavender, and she tested the heat with her foot before stepping into the bath, lowering herself.

Bliss was the first thought that slipped into her mind. Utter bliss. Evie lay back in the bath, sliding the soap through her fingers as she lathered it. She leaned forward, washing her shoulders before lying back and raising one leg to clean it. The terrible stench that had followed her from St. Giles was gone, and she was thankful for it. How anyone could throw such contents on an unsuspecting person was beyond her.

Her mind whirred with thoughts of the duke. Her hands slipped over her skin, and she closed her eyes, thinking of his hands on her flesh, teasing and caressing her body, clasping her breasts and kissing her nipples.

She sighed, wanting him in such a way. No one kissed someone as the duke kissed her. Not unless they were lovers or at least on the path of becoming so. The idea of taking the duke to her bed was not such a scandalous thought, not anymore at least. The night at the inn when he had laid upon her on the bed, his hardness teasing her wet flesh made her breathing hitch. Oh, to be back at the Bear Inn once again. Alone with the duke.

"Evie?"

The sound of his voice so close behind her rent a squeal from her and she sat forward in the water, covering herself. "Finn," she said, using his given name. "What are you doing here?"

"I apologize, I thought you would've been out of the bath by now."

She turned and noted he was just inside the door, and yet so lost in her own musings, she didn't hear him enter or close the door behind him.

"I was covered in human excrement. I may be a little while in the bath." Evie dipped into the water to try to cover her nakedness. A pointless exercise. She could see her nudity under the clear water, and she had little doubt that the duke could as well.

"I did consider it, and then I ignored that consideration."

Evie looked over her shoulder, meeting his gaze. She shivered at the longing she read in his blue orbs. He looked wretched, lost, and confused, and her heart did a little flip in her chest. The past few days had been some of the most enjoyable of her life. She could not understand why Lucy would throw over this wonderful, honorable man for someone else.

The duke was a catch to any woman, and yet he was in her room, alone, and she was naked. Her friends would be scandalized should they know the improper thoughts that were running through her mind. Of all the things that one could do with a man that no woman of intact virtue ought to know.

But she'd read enough books in her seven and twenty years to know what happened between a man and a woman. To do those things with the duke made her shiver and ache in places she'd never ached before.

She reached for the drying cloth on the nearby chair and standing, wrapped it around herself before turning toward the duke. "What do you really want, Finn?" she asked, not just for tonight, but always. Did he want a rich, noble wife to be his duchess, or would a woman from Wiltshire with no money and no connections satisfy his aristo-cratic blood?

"I want you," he said at length, striding across the room and hoisting her up in his arms. Evie gasped, letting go of her inhibitions and her towel and simply held on to him, wrapping her arms about his neck and kissing him as fiercely as he kissed her.

His clothing was rough against her nakedness, but changed now back into clothing that was suitable for a duke, his attire was soft and smelled fresh and clean. She wrapped herself about him, hooking her legs around his back and pressed her aching sex against his.

He moaned through their kiss, spinning her and walking backward toward the bed. He carried her as if she weighed nothing at all and deposited her on her bed. She bounced once, and she giggled.

The duke didn't move from the end of the bed, his gaze hungrily devouring her form. He ran a hand across his jaw before stripping off his coat and tearing at his cravat. "I want you. No one else. Only you."

His words sent a bolt of heat to lick up her spine, and hope bloomed in her chest. Did he truly mean it? She hoped that he did. She kneeled on the bed, reaching out to help him undress. She wanted him too, ached with the need of him.

Together, they stripped him of his jacket, waistcoat, and cravat, his articles of clothing pooling about his feet. The sight of his muscled chest made her mouth water. Evie ran her hand over the corded muscles that flexed under her touch and each ragged breath the duke took. Finn was warm, his heart beating a fast crescendo of need. She had done that. Made him want her, and no one else.

"We shouldn't do this, Evie." His words were breathless

and held a hint of regret in them. He was torn between doing what was right and expected of a gentleman and what they both wanted. And right now, Evie wanted him and be damned what etiquette they were breaking.

"You do not want me?" she teased, her hands dipping to his breeches to unhook the buttons keeping all of him from her.

He leaned his forehead against hers, his breath rasping against her face. "Damn it, yes, I want you, but we're not married. This is wicked."

Evie met his gaze as her fingers slipped the first button on his breeches free. "We're consenting adults, Finn. There is nothing wrong with what we're going to do." She needed this, even if for one night. To lose herself with a man who made her blood sing and her body yearn.

He raised one brow, not moving to push her hands away. "Are you sure you wish to do this?" he asked, his hand stemming hers as she undid one more of the buttons on his breeches.

"Oh yes, we're doing this," she replied, slipping the button free.

He leaned forward, kissing her neck. A shiver rocked through her, and she slid her hand inside his breeches, touching him for the first time. His manhood was ridged, long and wide, and yet the skin was the softest she'd ever felt before, like steel encased in velvet. His hand clasped over hers, showing her without words what he liked.

What she liked too.

"You enjoy that?" she asked, when he moaned, nipping the skin on her neck.

"Fuck yes," he groaned, the use of the word shocked and pleased her. He wasn't so much the proper duke. Not always. Not with her and not like this.

They tumbled onto the bed, and she slipped her legs about his waist, wanting the weight of him, his body against hers. His chest brushed her breasts, her nipples hard little peaks that ached for his touch. Evie pressed against him, wanting him to soothe the ache that he made.

"You're so beautiful," he said between kisses as he made his way down to her breasts, his tongue tasting her skin, his teeth giving sweet little bites along the way. She could lose herself in the arms of this man. Envy and jealousy rippled through her that he had been betrothed to her sister, that had Lucy not run away with another man, that right now it could be her sister in his arms.

Evie pushed the unhelpful, troubling thoughts aside. She would not think of such a horror. The duke was kissing her, had her beneath him in her bed within his home. She would fight for what she wanted, and she wanted him—all of him tonight and every night after.

She spiked her fingers through his hair as his mouth covered one nipple, his tongue laving at her sensitive flesh. Evie held on to him and let go of all her troubles, her secrets, and simply let herself enjoy.

Finn.

❧

*F*inn was going to hell and heaven from the feel of Evie beneath him. To seduce a woman only days after his betrothed had run off with another man was not the act of a gentleman. Yet nothing save a natural disaster would tear him away from Evie's delectable body right at this moment. Her breasts, in particular, were the perfect size for his hands.

Evie gasped his name, a husky pant that told him more

than anything that she enjoyed his touch. She rubbed against him, a siren stretch that pushed her soaking mons against his aching cock, and for a moment, his mind went blank. He pressed against her, giving her what they both wanted, and he fought not to guide himself into her sweet cunny.

"You're teasing me, Finn. Stop teasing me," she gasped, her fingers tangling into his hair and pulling a little.

Oh, how he loved the sound of his name on her lips. Of how she undulated, thrust, and kissed him with such abandonment, not caring that he was a duke, a wealthy peer of the realm. She saw him as a man who could give her pleasure and company. He would marry this woman once her sister was settled with Mr. Brown. He'd not always wanted a woman of similar age to his, but he could not see himself with anyone else but Evie. That she was from Wiltshire, his home county, and fulfilled all of his father's decree was not to be overlooked either.

He reached down between them, placing himself at the tip of her wet cunny and pushed into her heat. She was so warm and tight that he bit back a groan. Impatient minx that Evie was, she lifted her hips, pushing him a little farther into her. He gasped at the pleasure of it, fighting the urge to thrust all the way in.

"Damn it, Finn. Take me. I'm aching for you. Surely you can feel how much I want you."

"I feel it, love," he said, ignoring the endearment that slipped naturally from his lips. He was merely caught up in the moment, nothing more. He soothed the part of him that wanted to panic at such blandishment. She moved again, and this time he thrust into her, making her his. She threw her head back, moaning at his intrusion. Finn breathed deep, bracing himself and kissed her neck, taking his time to suckle on the little vein that ran down from her ear to her shoulder.

Her skin was sweet and smelled of springtime, of jasmine and delicious honeyed things. So good. He wanted to lick and taste her all over. He thrust deeper still, hoisting her legs high on his hips to take her fast and sure.

"Finn," she moaned, her hands sliding down his back to caress his ass. "Oh yes."

For a moment he lost all ability to think straight, he thrust hard and deep, giving her what she wanted, and he too. The slap of their skin sounded loud in the room, a symphony of desire or pleasure and the most satisfying sound he'd heard in an eon. He wasn't a rakehell, a rogue who slept his way through the widows of the ton, or the whores who plied their trades at Covent Garden. He'd kissed women, yes, had one mistress whom he'd parted with once he'd heard he had to find a wife and within sixty days, but never before had he wanted to please a woman as much as he wanted to please Evie.

Not just here and now with her beneath him, with him ruining her completely, but with other things too. He would make her his duchess. Some would say he was an ass to go from one sister to the other, but he was under a time constraint, and Lucy did choose another to be her husband. He couldn't marry someone of his ilk, of his rank or wealth, but nor did he want to. Not after getting to know Evie better.

He wanted her.

Evie rolled him onto his back and straddled him. Finn gasped, not having expected her to do such a thing.

"I want to try it this way." She wiggled a little on his cock, and he sucked in a breath, fighting the urge to come.

She stilled above him. "Oh, I did not hurt you, did I, Finn?"

God no she did not. There was no pain between them, only pleasure, satisfying pleasure ripping through him. "No, not at all. By all means, please continue."

Her palms pushed down against his chest, and she levered herself up and down on him, sending his wits to spiral. He had not expected her to be so astute or so adventurous for her first time. Not that he was complaining, he would take all and everything that she offered him.

His cock was like steel, his balls ached with the need to spend, and the sight of her breasts rocking above his face did little to stem his desire to fuck her, take what he wanted until he shot his seed deep into her.

Finn clasped her hips, anchoring her to him and helped her to ride his cock. She fell into a rhythm, and he bit the side of his mouth, trying to stem his release. "Fuck that feels good," he said, thrusting into her each time she slipped down onto him.

Their joining became frantic, and then the most perfect, most beautiful sight he'd ever beheld in his life blossomed above him. Evie threw back her head, moaning his name as her sex tightened and contracted about his cock, pulling his release to mix with hers.

He spent his load, enjoyed her milking him of every little ounce before she slumped onto his chest, the beat of her heart coinciding with his.

"Well," she gasped, her head nestled under his chin. He felt the lightest kiss on his chest, and he closed his eyes, reveling in her touch. "That was simply exquisite and something that I do believe I'd enjoy doing again."

He chuckled, rolling her to the side of him before hoisting her up against his body, keeping her close. "Do you now," he said, teasing her and knowing full well that now that he'd had her once, he would have her again. And again, and possibly again after that before he had to return to his room in the morning.

"Oh yes," she said, glancing up at him. This close, he could see her luminescent brown orbs and the little flecks of copper in them. Something in his chest thumped hard, and he reached out, slipping a piece of her hair behind her ear that had fallen over one eye.

"Well then, as a gentleman, you know that I can deny you nothing. If that is your wish, then I am at your command."

A wicked little grin slipped onto her delectable mouth, a mouth he would never get tired of kissing, he was sure. "Hmm, at my command. How much I like to hear those words. I shall keep you accountable to your offer, Finn."

He leaned down, unable not to taste her again. Their kiss lingered, heated, and his cock stirred. Damn it, he was a rascal. He'd just deflowered a virgin. He could not have her again so soon. He ought to be horsewhipped.

"Please do, I look forward to a repeat performance."

"As do I," she said, kissing him anew and stripping him of all sense and gentlemanly manners.

~

*E*vie woke the next morning late, turned to glance at Finn and found nothing but a cold bed and linen that was decidedly empty of one gentleman duke. She sat up, glancing about her room. The small table before the fire was set with a delicious-looking breakfast of warm bread, ham, and eggs. A pot of tea steamed, all but begging her to the table. Evie pushed the blankets aside, slipped a shift over her naked self, and started toward the table.

The fire, newly stoked, radiated warmth. Evie smiled down at the food, knowing Finn had not been long in here, looking after her after their night of bliss. A night she was decidedly hopeful would be repeated often.

How wonderful it was to be in his arms, to be loved and caressed, adored, and kissed until she did not think she could bear much more of it. Evie sat on the chair closest to the fire and picked up the pot of tea, pouring herself a cup, adding a drop of milk just as she liked. That he'd had sent up such a delicious breakfast for her told her more than anything else that he cared.

Could his caring for her lead to more? That she did not know, but she was an always optimistic person, and she would fight to make him like her as much as she feared she was starting to like him.

The door to her room opened and in Finn walked. Dressed in tan breeches and blue jacket, he had forgone a waistcoat and simply wore a shirt and cravat. His hair still damp from his wash that morning. "Good morning," she said, unable to hold back the little grin his presence brought forth on her face.

He tipped her chin up with his hand, leaning down as if to kiss her. Her blood heated at his nearness and the thought of repeating everything they had done the night before flittered through her mind.

"Good morning, Evie," he said, placing a soft and too-short a kiss on her lips.

He sat across from her, spooning a hefty serving of ham, bacon, and eggs onto his plate and pouring himself a cup of tea."

"I have a proposition for you." His voice held a hint of

trepidation, and Evie met his gaze, wondering what he was thinking.

"What sort of proposition?" she asked, the idea that he'd ask her to be his mistress souring the taste of her tea in her mouth.

"I want you to be my wife."

CHAPTER 14

*E*vie stood in the front drawing room of the duke's townhouse, staring at the busy Mayfair street beyond and thinking of Lucy. Where was she? Was she safe? Was she married? She stayed behind the sheer curtains so no one could see her and thought of what they would do next. How they would find Lucy and ensure her marriage before it was too late. How to stop her from ruining herself beyond repair.

If she wasn't already.

"Pacing and chewing off your fingernails is not going to make Lucy appear before you, Evie. Come away and join me for tea," the duke said, standing from behind his desk and going to where the butler had not long left a tray of tea and sweet biscuits.

"They could have left for Scotland by now," she said, turning toward him. "We may have missed our chance here in London."

"We have not. I have men watching the White Horse Cellar Coaching Inn. I will know within the hour if they pass through there."

"What if they travel north by other means? Whatever will we do then?"

"They will not," Finn said, coming over to her and taking her hand, moving her toward the settee to have a cup of tea. "Everyone travels through the White Horse. They will, as well."

A ruckus in the foyer sounded, and Evie glanced at Finn as the distinct sound of her sister's voice rose above that of the butlers. "That's Lucy," she said, standing and all but running to the front door.

"Lucy," she called, not believing that her sister was here. At the duke's home, safe and well. Lucy stilled, turning toward her, relief replacing the ire on her usually pretty visage.

"Evie," she said, her shoulders slumping in relief. "You are here. Oh," she sighed. "I'm so glad."

Evie closed the space between them, and the nearer she came to her younger sister, the more she noticed her disheveled appearance. Gone was the clean, pressed gowns, her hair always up and in perfect order, even her face had little smudges of grime upon it.

"Lucy, I'm so happy to see you." Evie pulled her into a tight embrace, and she could feel her sister's tension in the line of her back. "What has happened? You're upset. I can see it."

Her sister's eyes filled with tears, and Evie walked her back toward the drawing room, Finn stepping aside as they came into the room. "Come, have a cup of tea. It looks like you're in need of sustenance."

"Oh, Evie." Her sister hiccupped, the tears falling down her cheeks unheeded. "I've been such a fool, and I fear when I tell you what has happened, you'll never forgive me, or the duke."

The mention of Finn did little to help Evie's nerves. The fact that her sister was also without her betrothed or husband was also of great concern. They made their way inside the drawing room, and Finn closed the door, giving them privacy from himself and the staff.

Evie pulled Lucy to sit beside her on the settee, pouring her a cup of tea and handing it to her. That her sister was without Mr. Brown left Evie with an uncertain, sinking type of feeling in her stomach. If Lucy was not married, then she was ruined. This was not what she had hoped for her vibrant, enthusiastic sister.

"What happened, Lucy? Tell me everything. Where is Mr. Brown?"

"Oh, Evie," her sister said, wailing into a fit of tears, her teacup rattling on its plate. "It's all such a mess. I made a complete muddle of everything." Lucy sniffed, and Evie reached into her pocket, passing her a handkerchief. Another oddity as Lucy always carried a handkerchief, and anything else she thought one would require during any situation.

"You know that I ran off with Mr. Brown, Anthony, and all was going splendidly, but when we arrived in London two days ago, he ran into some friends from Bath, and everything changed. We were staying at a lodging house in St. Giles, and he started to go out at night, leaving me behind. Saying that it wasn't correct that I should join him if we were not married, and so I did not. But then last night, he returned, well into his cups and…"

"He did not force you, did he, Lucy?" The idea that her sister was assaulted wasn't a thought she ever wanted to contemplate, and Mr. Brown would want to be many miles from here if he so much as touched one strand of hair on Lucy's head.

"No, no, nothing like that, I assure you, but he did return, declared that he was going to travel abroad with his friends. I thought he was a farmer, settled and happy in Wiltshire. Whatever happened to his love of the land or his county or his love for me for that matter?"

"And so you have not married him?" Evie squeezed Lucy's hand when she did not reply, although, by her pale countenance and a red nose from too much crying, Evie already knew the answer to her question.

"We did not marry. He left me this morning, and I used the last of my money to travel here to the duke's home. I knew, you see, that you were looking for me. I saw you yesterday walking the streets in St. Giles, and I'm sorry, Evie, but I hid from you."

"Lucy, we were only trying to ensure Mr. Brown did the right thing and married you. We were not going to send you home if you did not wish it."

"I know," she said, tipping her head down. "I tried to return home via coach, but I only had enough funds to make Mayfair. I was going to write to Mama and Papa to send someone to collect me, but now that you are here, I am saved."

Evie sighed, wishing that were true, but her sister had not thought too much about her circumstances or what they meant for her. Circumstances that Evie thankfully would not need to worry about herself since the duke had asked for her hand. Evie had promised him she would marry him once her sister was married and settled. To see Lucy now unmarried and decidedly ruined was not what she'd wanted to face.

"The duke wanted to ensure that you were married. Papa sent us to follow you, you see. You will have to return home, and in time, hopefully, the scandal will pass."

Lucy glanced about the room, taking in its decorative walls covered in silk wallpaper, the many books, and marble fireplace. A smile spread across her pretty face. "I will not be ruined, Evie. The duke coming after me proves that he cares. I shall simply marry him instead."

Evie stilled at her sister's words. Marry the duke? What was her sister thinking!

"The Duke of Carlisle is with me to ensure Mr. Brown did the right thing and married you. Now that he has not, all that can be done is to bring you home and try to limit any scandal. Fortunately, our family is not well-known in town, and you may escape too much social shaming."

Lucy patted her tears away with Evie's handkerchief, her countenance brightening with each minute. "I went with Mr. Brown because I thought the duke did not care for me as much as Mr. Brown did. But I was wrong. He's come after me, no doubt, to try to stop my betrothal. I had thought that he was merely offering for my hand because I was there and of age, but I think that estimation was incorrect."

"What are you saying?" Evie asked, the pit of her stomach churning, the room spinning at her feet.

"There will be no scandal, Evie, for I'll marry the duke. To society he is still my betrothed. He's a gentleman," Lucy continued, "he would not cry off from an under-standing, not when contracts have been signed."

Evie swallowed, unsure she was capable of words right at this moment. "You wish to marry the duke? Still? I do not think that is an option, Lucy." A terrible thought, but Evie could not allow the duke to marry her sister. Not now, not after she had given herself to him. Had fallen in love with him and she hoped, with all her heart, that he too was in love with her. He had asked for her hand in marriage after all. There had to be affection between them.

"Of course, he shall have me, Evie." Lucy laughed, but even Evie could hear the nervous tone to her words. "You will see. His honor and his hatred of scandal will ensure such an outcome."

Evie did not wish to see that at all, and she was a terrible person to think that about her sister. Over the past several days that they had spent together, she had come to respect and care for the duke. He was a good man, sweet and amusing, and, as Lucy said, honorable.

Knowing that the woman he betrothed himself to had not married, had, in fact, made an error of judgment, would he marry her still? If he was to do such a thing, what did that mean for her? What was she going to do if the man she loved married her sister?

"You will have to speak to the duke, but you ran off with another man, Lucy. It is unlikely he will forgive such folly and marry you still. While he came after you to ensure that your reputation was kept intact and that you had not made a mistake, I do not believe he will allow you to be his wife."

"Why are you not helping me? Defending me? The way you speak, you sound as if you do not wish for me to become a duchess at all." Lucy stood, going to the window and looking out past the curtains. "I did care for the duke, you know. I may not have loved him, but I did agree to be his wife."

"You also asked me to seduce him away from you. Have you forgotten so quickly what you were willing to ask me to do so you could marry your Mr. Brown?"

Lucy turned, staring at her with innocent, widened eyes. It was as if she had forgotten her request and was now scandalized by it. Whatever was her sister up to? "Please tell me you did not. You know that I only said that in jest. I would never want you to throw yourself at the duke for my sake. You did not, did you, Evie? You did not seduce my betrothed away from me."

Evie took a calming breath as the world around her started to spiral out of control. "Lucy, I never seduced the duke away from you." Which was true. When they had finally come together, it was mutual and with the understanding that Lucy would be married by the time they caught up to the eloping pair. The duke had long thought his understanding to her sister over. Lucy's actions had ensured that. They had done nothing wrong. Evie did not set out to break her sister's engagement. Lucy had done that herself. To now turn about and chastise her, beg her to tell her something that she did not want to hear, even if she had asked her to do so in the first place was unfair. All of this was unfair.

"Of course, I did not take it as a jest, but I did not seduce him away from you, Lucy. You left him for another man. You were going to marry Mr. Brown."

A knock on the door sounded, and Evie stood, going to open it. The duke stood on the threshold, his gaze slipping over her shoulder to her sister, who sat in the room beyond. Evie stepped back, opening the door wider so he could enter. The duke glanced across the room, and like a shutter on a window, his demeanor changed. He stood straight, the smile wiped from his handsome visage and replaced with that of the duke's, all proper and schooled.

"Miss Lucy, good of you to join us."

Lucy burst into another pool of tears and stood, running over to the duke, throwing herself into his arms. She wrapped her hands about his back, holding steadfast.

"Oh, Your Grace. You've saved me. I'm so very sorry. Mr. Brown led me to believe that he loved me and that I was special. I was a fool to follow him. He is the worst of people. Please tell me you forgive me. Tell me that I have not lost your affection."

Evie closed the door. As much as she loved her sister, had always protected her from the world, her actions right at this moment reeked of a spoiled, rotten child. What was her sister thinking throwing herself at the duke as if he was free to marry her still? At least, Evie hoped he was not free, or her hopes and dreams with him were over.

"You're not married?" the duke asked, setting Lucy away from him a little, holding her at arm's length. The sight of Lucy in the duke's embrace did not sit well, and Evie narrowed her eyes, all hope that there may be a future for her and the duke slowly dissipating before her very eyes.

"I made a mistake. I was tricked, you see. Mr. Brown was not who I thought he was. Please tell me that I have not lost you. As a gentleman, I know that you would not leave me to the wolves."

Evie watched with horror as Lucy stared up at Finn, her eyes filling with tears. She looked crestfallen and lost, in need of support. Evie should want to help her, and she did, truly, but she did not want her to have Finn. She had chosen Mr. Brown. Was supposed to be at this very moment married to him. Not standing before the very man she loved and adored asking for him to honor his marriage proposal.

Finn stared down at Lucy, seemingly lost for words. Evie willed him to tell Lucy no. No, he would not marry her, not after being thrown over for another.

"You signed contracts to marry me, Your Grace," Lucy

said, using his title for the first time since she'd seen him again. "I know I have done you wrong, and I promise never to be persuaded elsewhere in the future, but I do not wish to bring scandal down on my family if I can help it. And your family too," she added, walking over to Evie and picking up her hand. "Is that not right, my dear? Both His Grace's and our family will be forever talked about should we not marry."

"The banns have not been called as yet, Lucy. No one need ever know that the duke offered for you."

"Oh, well, after Mr. Brown left me last evening, I wrote to Papa and asked him to announce our betrothal. I do hope you do not mind, Your Grace. With the contracts signed, your honor, and my apology, I did hope that we could marry and have a happy life together. Just as we planned."

Evie stared at Lucy and was unable to believe what she was hearing. Had her sister gone mad? To think the duke could just forgive her after her indiscretion was absurd.

"You had the banns called?" Finn met Evie's gaze, and she saw the disappointment within them. A disappointment that she too felt.

"Lucy, how could you do that to the duke?"

Her sister gave a nervous laugh, and yet Evie could not see anything amusing in the situation.

"How could I not?" Lucy looked between them, her eyes narrowing in thought. "The duke is in London trying to catch up with me, is he not? No doubt because he still cares for me and wants to marry me. I am sorry for the trouble I have caused. I do wish to marry His Grace if he will have me. You will have me, won't you, Finn?"

"I, ahh," he mumbled, looking at Evie, somewhat stricken.

"Lucy, will you please leave us? I wish to speak to His Grace alone. Ask the butler in the foyer to take you to your room."

Lucy looked between them, before nodding and, without another word, started for the door, but not before stopping beside Evie.

"Please help me convince the duke, Evie. I know you love me and will do this for me because we're sisters and have always supported each other. I truly am sorry for all the trouble I caused."

Evie walked Lucy to the door, closing it behind her sister without another word before rounding on the duke. "You cannot marry Lucy. I love her, I do. She's my sister, and I will do everything to protect her, but this? No, not this."

"The scandal will be atrocious, for both our families if I do not make right on my proposal and marry her."

"I think after what she has done, and you as well, Finn that be damned the scandal. What about us? What about the offer of your hand to me?"

The duke ran a hand through his hair, pacing before the hearth. "It never occurred to me that she would not be married. I had hoped we could marry once we were satisfied that Miss Lucy was settled with Mr. Brown, but it does not seem to be the case. No matter how much we may dislike the situation, I am, in fact, betrothed to your sister."

"And you ruined me," she said, unable to hold back that truth, even though she hated saying the words. It was not the duke's fault that they had fallen into bed together. It was just as much Evie's fault as it was his. A mutual desire that was acted upon.

"I must marry, Evie, and I'm running out of time to do so. If your sister holds me to the understanding, it is her that I must marry. No matter how much I wished it would be you."

She took a calming breath, thinking on his words before recollecting what he said. "What do you mean you're running out of time to marry? Are you ill and must beget an heir before your time runs out?" The thought made her want to cast up her accounts. She could not bear it if Finn were sick.

"No," he sighed, running a hand through his hair. "I am not sick. What I have failed to tell you is that my father decreed in his will that if I were not married a year after his passing, I had only sixty days to do so, or I would lose monetary funds that are required to run Stoneheim Palace and my other properties."

Evie paused at his words, his hasty actions in securing her sister's hand finally making sense. "You offered to marry Lucy because you did not wish to lose your inheritance?"

"I did," he said, pacing still, his hair further on end.

"You could have married anyone. Why my sister?"

"Father had also decreed in his will that I must marry a woman from my home county and who was a gentleman's daughter. Your family met my requirements." The duke sat, staring at the fire, lost in thought.

"Why did you not think of me as your prospective wife when you first called on Papa?" They had known each other in London after all. Granted, they did not know each other well, but they had mutual friends, circulated within the same social sphere, to choose her sister seemed odd to Evie. Or, perhaps, he had not desired her in that way. The thought left a hollow feeling deep in her core.

"Because you're my age. I'm a duke. I require a wife

who will give me an heir. I feared that your age would be an impediment to this."

Evie felt her mouth pop open at his words, and for a moment, she was unable to respond. She was too old? There was no mistake that she was older than Lucy, a few good years in fact, but she was not yet eight and twenty. Women older than her were still having children. Why Ava had a child only last year, and she was two years older than Evie. What had he been thinking?

"So why offer for me if during this whole time I was too much of a crone for your exacting standards."

The duke looked up from his chair, understanding dawning on his face. He stood and came over to her, reaching for her hands. Evie stepped out of his reach, wanting to know the truth. All of it, even if it were as ugly as her sister's actions from earlier today.

"You know I care for you, Evie. We've been intimate. It would be wrong of me not to offer for you."

"But you cannot now, can you? You're already betrothed to my sister and now that she will be ruined should you not marry her, create a scandal which you loathe to endure, I am left alone. Left looking like the biggest fool in history, but I shall survive," she said, rallying herself not to cry. "I am, after all, a woman and capable of weathering any storm."

"I want you. You know that I do," he said, reaching for her. Evie moved farther away from him.

"Do not fear, Your Grace. Society would never imagine such a virile, powerful duke such as yourself would waste his time with a woman who was of his age. How uncomely and vulgar."

"Evie, that is not true, and you know it."

She shrugged, heading toward the door. "None of it

matters now. You require a wife, and your betrothed is now yours once more. She's young and will give you heirs. I may not. Not to mention your dislike of scandal will be averted should you do as you originally planned."

"Evie," he said, coming over to her and turning her to look at him. "We've been intimate. I cannot abandon you."

"I have always put my sister above anyone else, cared, and looked out for her her whole life. I'm not about to let her fall on her own sword. Even if that was of her own making. You will marry her, and I shall be fine. We will not speak of this time again, and from the moment I walk out of this house, what has passed between us is to be forgotten. Do you agree?"

He stared down at her, his beautiful, aristocratic face that she had kissed with abandon no longer going to be hers to have. A lump lodged in her throat, and she tried to swallow past it.

"How are we to go on as if nothing has happened between us? I cannot marry your sister under such circumstances. It would not be right."

"You will tell her nothing. You cannot. To do so will ruin my reputation and hers because she would call off the wedding if she knew the truth."

"Evie," he said, frowning, his hands tight upon her shoulders. "How will I stay away from you?"

"Because your family has been through enough scandal to last it two lifetimes, you said so yourself. You will have a happy marriage with my sister and will keep your distance from me because you have to. That is how you will stay away from me."

A muscle worked at his temple before he stepped back, the chasm between them growing wider and wider by the minute. "I will return to my London home with Lucy.

Mama and Papa can travel to London for the wedding. Your nuptials must be seen as a joyous and much-celebrated event. A marriage all the way in Wiltshire will not do."

The duke nodded but said nothing, merely watched her. "I'm sorry, Evie," he whispered.

Evie walked to the door, hoping that the duke would stop her, while all the while praying that he did not. They could never be. Not now, at least. "I'm sorry too," she said at the door, before she opened it and left him behind her.

Evie went upstairs and packed her things, explaining the situation to Lucy before heading out the front of the duke's townhouse and hiring a hackney cab. Leaving her heart inside.

CHAPTER 15

inn started to make the usual circulations that were required of him whenever he was in town, and the Season was in full swing. He'd attended numerous balls, had played the doting fiancée, and yet he'd never been more sorry for himself.

How on earth was he to marry Miss Lucy when Evie was in the world, an impossibility that he could not stomach. The past three weeks had been torture. To parade a woman about town as if they were the happiest couple in England made him want to cast up his accounts. Made him want to storm across the ballroom floor right this instant and demand Evie to see sense. To forget what everyone thought, what scandal his marrying her instead of her sister would create and live a long and happy life together.

He wanted her back. Hated that she'd reverted to the proper English lady who was courteous, commandeering, and sweet—helping her sister prepare for the wedding and only too happy to give him and Miss Lucy time together whenever he called. He didn't go to her London home to see his betrothed. God forgive him, he went there to see Evie.

Finn stood beside his friend, the Duke of Whitstone, sipping a whiskey while His Grace watched the Duchess of Whitstone dance a minuet with Viscount Duncannon.

"Miss Lucy will make a sweet wife for you, Finn. I will admit to being surprised to hear you're marrying the younger Milton girl. I always thought you and the elder Miss Milton suited better in temperament. At least, when we've been together in London, that is what I gathered."

Finn was well aware that he suited Evie better than anyone ever before in his life. Hell, even now, as he spied Evie across the room, speaking to her group of friends, laughing and smiling, he was conscious of how much he missed her.

Loved her.

The past three weeks in town had been hell. Sleep eluded him. It would seem that he could no longer rest alone, missed having her beside him, someone to reach over and pull into his embrace whenever he wished.

He drank down the last of his whiskey, steeling himself to speak the words that he'd tried not to these past days. "I've made a grave error, and I do not know how to fix my circumstance."

The duke glanced at him, his brow furrowing. "Tell me everything. Perhaps I can assist you," Whitstone said, watching him with something akin to pity. As if he suspected already that he longed for Evie instead of his betrothed Miss Lucy.

Finn sighed, hating himself beyond measure right at this moment. Whatever was he going to do? "I have offered to the wrong sister, and now there is little I can do about it."

The duke nodded, turning back to watch the dancers on the floor. "I know something of what happened between you and Evie. Ava has disclosed some particulars. Whatever made you agree to marry Miss Lucy after she threw you over for another man? You are not obliged to marry her after she treated you with so little respect."

"I know I am not, but she had written to her father, asking for the banns to be called after her Mr. Brown high-tailed it to the Continent. Not to mention, she begged Evie to help her in gaining back her betrothed. Should I have called it off, the scandal would've been great. All of London would've talked about my name for months. I could not endure that again."

"And so, you'll endure a lifetime of misery in a marriage you do not want?" the duke scoffed, before clearing his throat. "If you believed Miss Milton that she is content with this decision, you're fooling yourself. A woman in love does not want her love to marry her sibling."

Hearing it spoken out loud made his blood run cold. It also left him wondering why the hell he'd agreed to such an action. Miss Lucy had no feelings for him or respect by what she had done, whereas he had an overwhelming notion that what he felt for Evie, was something that he could not live the rest of his life without. He cared for her deeply. More than he'd ever cared for anyone else in his life. Her opinion was what he valued most, and so when she demanded he save her sister's reputation, he could not deny her.

"You think that Evie loves me still?" Finn closed his eyes a moment, needed to break his view of Evie across the other side of the room. "I do not know how I'm to keep myself from her. To think of all the times ahead of us that she will visit Lucy at Stoneheim Palace. Have Seasons with us here in town, and I'm to be distant, unaffected by her presence. It's an impossible thing to ask of a man."

"An impossible thing to ask a man who is in love."

Love?

The word reverberated around in his mind once again and he fought not to panic at the decision that he had to make. His marriage was to take place next week. How could he go through with such a thing? He could not, but did that mean he loved Evie? Finn looked to where she stood with her companions, just as she glanced up and stared in his direction. Their eyes met. Held. Time stilled, and the music drifted away, and all that was left in the room was the two of them.

Regret, savage, and brutal, tore through him, and he fought not to stride across the ballroom floor and take her in his arms, tell her that he was sorry. That he'd made a mistake, not just in London but when in Marlborough too. That he should have thought to ask her to be his bride. He'd always liked Evie, had known her through their mutual friends, why he'd allowed his narrow-minded views on women and their age to impinge on his decision he could not fathom. A mistake that he would forever regret, but at least he could do something now about it. Before it was too late.

She turned back to her friends, severing their contact, and the action cut him like a blade. Finn summoned a footman, in need of another drink. "How does a duke cry off from a wedding? Tell me, Whitstone, how I have managed to get myself into this position? My father was the man who London watched and gossiped about for his antics, never me. How have I allowed this to happen?"

Whitstone clapped him on the shoulder. "We are

human, Finn. We may be dukes, but we do make mistakes. Take myself and Ava. I lost her for years because I followed my parents' decree and believed them their lies. Do you think you should accept Miss Lucy's lies, her treatment of you, and lose the only woman you've ever loved? You cannot and you do not need me to tell you that for you already know what is right. Be damned the scandal that it will cause. You're the Duke of Carlisle. Who is to naysay or ridicule you? No one."

Finn thought over Whitstone's words, knowing them for the truth that they were. His friend was right, of course. He could not marry Miss Lucy. He did not love her, nor could he marry a woman who had run off with another man, no matter what crying off from their wedding would do to her reputation. She cared naught for him when she had chosen Mr. Brown.

His gaze landed on Evie once more, and warmth seeped into his bones for the first time since she had left his townhouse three weeks ago. He could not marry Miss Lucy, not when he loved Evie.

Loved her so very much that all he could think about was to make things right, to have her in his arms and love her for the rest of his days to the best of his ability.

"You're right," he said to Whitstone, a weight lifting from his shoulders at the sound of those words aloud. "I will make things right, and I will marry the woman I love. Not the woman whom I'm betrothed to."

"Good man," Whitstone said, taking a whiskey from a footman and clicking his glass against Finn's. "Congratulations on your forthcoming marriage. I know you shall be very happy. You will not regret this choice."

Finn smiled, sipping the amber liquid. "I believe I shall not. To love," he said, toasting the emotion.

"To love," Whitstone agreed, smiling at their antics.

~

The following afternoon Evie sat in the front parlor of the London home she shared with Molly, her parents were seated before the fire, discussing Lucy's marriage next week. Evie tried to ignore their chatter, their excitement that their youngest daughter was marrying one of the wealthiest, most highly situated men in England.

Evie had already decided what she would do once her sister was married, and Molly had agreed to go with her. They would travel abroad, visit Europe and see all the beautiful things that they had never seen before.

She could not stay in England to see her sister start her life with the man Evie loved. She could not. To do so would be the veriest torture, not to mention impossible to bear. The last three weeks that they had been in town had been unbearable. To watch her sister hang off the duke, play and tease him as if she had never run off with Mr. Brown had changed her opinion of her sister forever.

Of course, she would always love her, but she no longer respected her so much. How she could do such a thing to the duke, a good man, not faultless by any means, but still a good man overall, was beyond her.

Her stomach twisted, and the ever-present nausea wracked her. She had been progressing more and more each day with illness. Her trip abroad could not come soon enough. She needed to get away from seeing the duke and Lucy together. It was making her unwell.

Or something was.

There would be other adventures in her life, other

gentlemen admirers, and perhaps even a man who would love her as much as she feared she loved the duke.

The door to the parlor opened, and their butler announced the Duke of Carlisle.

Evie stood, curtsying as he entered before sitting back down. Her parents stood, going to the duke and fussing over him for several minutes. During their conversation, Lucy joined them, her golden locks bounding about her shoulders, her pretty blue eyes throwing the duke a coquettish look whenever she thought he was watching her.

Evie glanced back down at the knitting in her lap. She should have guessed that he would call this afternoon, he called every afternoon. She should have gone to her room or disappeared in the upstairs parlor, but she had not. Her foolish heart lived for his visits, to hear his deep, seductive voice speak of nothing of import for an hour or so before taking his leave.

The times with him here reminded her of when they were together on their travels to town. That time seemed a million years ago now, and never to be repeated. She could not wait until she left for Europe with Molly. No longer could she call London or Wiltshire home. Not if that meant she would have to see almost weekly her sister's happiness that came at the price of her own.

Her stomach cramped, and she stilled, hoping she would not be ill in front of everyone. Her travels abroad could not come soon enough for another reason as well. This very morning she had visited a doctor on Harley Street, and she'd been informed that she was with child.

Evie clutched her stomach, a sense of rightness, and also fear, filling her. Molly said she would help her abroad with the baby and help her on their return home to settle her somewhere in the country. A plan they were going to be discussing with the Duchess of Whitstone when she arrived shortly.

As if the very thought of Ava conjured her, she waltzed into the room, as pretty as ever, greeting everyone.

"Good afternoon," she said, smiling at those present before coming over to Evie. "I'm so very sorry to do this to you all, but I must beg a private audience with Evie. Please do excuse us."

Ava clasped Evie's hand and pulled her from the room, heading for the upstairs parlor. "What is it that's so important? When I received Molly's missive, it left me fearing the worse. Are you ill?"

"I will explain everything when we're alone." Evie took Ava into the private parlor and was glad to find Molly already in the room, reading a book. Evie checked for servants before shutting and locking the door. She leaned against the wood, knowing the best way to announce her news was to the point and without any hesitation.

"I'm pregnant with the Duke of Carlisle's baby."

Molly, as expected, did not react. The duchess, however, stood from her chair, her mouth agape but without any words. "Tell me that is not true. Evie. Surely you are joking." Ava looked between them and slowly lowered herself back onto her seat when Evie and Molly remained quiet.

Evie came to sit with them both. "Please do not be cross, Ava, you're making me more nervous than I already am."

Ava stared at her, her usually perfect brow marred with a scowl. "He's marrying your sister next week. You have not forgotten that have you, my dear?"

How could she forget? Had she not been carrying the duke's child, she may have learned to live with her sister's marriage to the man she loved, and she did love him. More than she'd ever thought to love anyone in her life. She had thought marriage, courtship, and affection would never be hers to have, but she'd been wrong. With the duke, she had all of those things, and now he was marrying someone else.

"That is why I'm traveling to Europe above anything else, even though I've longed to return to France and visit other locales. We shall stay away for a good year before returning home."

"What shall you do when you return to England? I think if you're carrying a child about with you, people will notice. The duke and your sister above anyone else."

"That is where you come in, I hope," she said, steeling herself to ask for help. She wasn't used to having to be reliant on anyone for anything, but she would need the help of her friends if she were to survive this change in her circumstance.

"Me? What would you like me to do?" Ava asked.

"We need you to see if you have an empty cottage that Evie can live in on your estate. Away from society, but close to a community that she may be able to bring up her child without the censure of anyone we know," Molly said, answering for Evie.

Ava did not reply for several moments. "Well, of course, I shall help you, but I will not lie to Whitstone, and so he will know the reason as to why I'm hiding you on our property."

Evie could understand that well enough and nodded. "Very well, so long as His Grace does not tell anyone of my whereabouts or why I have disappeared from society. They do not need to know, and the Duke of Carlisle certainly does not need to know."

"Hmm," Ava said, narrowing her eyes on Evie. "Are you certain about that choice? If you told Carlisle of your circumstance, I think you would find that he would break off his engagement with Lucy and marry you. You do love him, do you not? Why not fight for him instead of running away to Europe?"

"Could you imagine what society would think if they found out what I had done. To them, I slept with my sister's betrothed and fell pregnant with his child. I cannot let anyone know what I have done, not if I'm to protect the child I'm carrying from being labeled a bastard, among other things."

"People will ask questions. Are you prepared for those?" Ava asked.

"I will have some months to prepare myself for those questions while we're in Europe. If I have to see my family or Lucy and her husband, I shall ensure my child is safe at home, and I shall only visit sparingly. I cannot see them together. Even to imagine Finn lost to me forever is a pain that I cannot bear."

"You love him so very much, Evie. Please tell him the truth. I know the duke shied away from society, the gossip and scandals all because his father was normally the very one who created them, but he would throw all of that aside if he knew that you were having his baby. He loves you, I'm sure, and does not wish to marry Lucy. You really ought to give him the opportunity to choose."

"I did give him the opportunity to choose, and because of my sister's scheming, her reminder of the scandal, the duke chose her. No child in my womb should alter his choice. He either wishes to be with me, or he does not."

"He does love you, though," Molly said. "The other night at Lord and Lady Hood's ball, I watched him most of the evening. He did little but stare at you, his eyes following you about the room like you were the only woman present."

"I know the duke cares for me, but he has chosen to honor his understanding with Lucy, and no matter what Lucy has done, I do love her and never wish to see her shunned by society. Not simply because she was fooled by a man who lied to her."

"I like your sister too, Evie, but she chose to run away. Had her beau not run away, she would already be married to him. The duke and yourself need to remember that when you're deciding to live separate lives. Why should you both suffer the consequences of someone else? Yes, Carlisle should not have offered to Lucy, but neither did she have to agree to his offer when all along she was in love with someone else."

"And had no intention of marrying the duke," Molly put in, her lips pursed.

"What do you mean by that?" Ava asked, looking at Molly before turning to Evie.

Evie sighed, knowing Ava deserved to know the whole truth. "The night before Lucy ran away with Mr. Brown, she asked me to seduce the duke, or at least convince the duke that he'd made a mistake in asking for her hand. She asked me to help her break off the understanding in some way."

Ava gasped, her hand clutching the pearls about her neck. "Tell me this is not true. Your sister asked this of you, and you're still willing to let her marry the man you love and who loves you in return. I cannot allow their marriage to occur. It would be a mistake and one they both will pay the price for the moment they're expected to consummate the marriage."

The idea of Lucy sleeping with the duke made Evie's stomach turn, and she took a calming breath. "All that you say is true, I know that, but it doesn't change anything. The duke may love me as much as I love him, but he offered to Lucy first, and now she is in need of his name to save her reputation. I will not stand in the way of that."

"You also need the duke's name to save your reputation, Evie. And if you think for one moment that Carlisle will be pleased that you did not tell him that you're carrying his child, you are acting a bigger fool than you already are."

"Ava," Evie said, a shard of hurt piercing her heart at her friend's words. "That is unkind."

"I'm being honest. Carlisle will hate the fact that his child is now illegitimate because you did not tell him the truth. He will find out, Evie. The truth always has a way of coming out."

"That is very true," Molly said, nodding in agreement.

Evie looked between her friends. They meant well, but Lucy was her sister. How could she ruin her sister's only chance of keeping her reputation intact? No one knew outside their friend set that Evie had been intimate with the duke, loved him beyond reason. Her reputation was safe, so long as she could disappear into the wilds of England with her baby somewhere, never to return.

"I know what you're saying, and I love you for your honesty, truly I do." Evie reached out and clasped both of her friends' hands, squeezing them a little. "But I have made up my mind, and I'm determined to allow the duke and Lucy to continue on with their plans for a future together. I will be happy to remove myself from society and not be in anyone's way."

Ava shook her head, her lips pulled into a disapproving,

thin line. "I do not agree with this. You're Evie, our impulsive, fun, determined friend. You ought to fight for your heart and happy future."

"I may have lost the duke," Evie said, loving her friends for their support and honesty. "But I shall not be heartbroken. I will have a little part of him when our child is born, and that child will be my greatest love. A sign that what we had together was real, even if it were only fleeting."

Molly sighed, smiling wistfully. "That is truly lovely, but we still do not agree. You need to tell the duke the truth and now, before it's too late."

"I agree," Ava put in. "And if you do not, Evie Milton, be warned, that I shall."

CHAPTER 16

innf paced Earl Tinley's drawing room at His Lordship's yearly ball, the muffled sounds of music and conversation seeping into the room. The ball was far from an enjoyable night out, it was a crush out there, too many people in attendance, the stifling heat from the compacted bodies and the numerous odors were enough to make him want to leave, get on his horse, and return to Wiltshire.

He swore, running a hand through his hair. Tomorrow was his wedding day. A day that he could not go through with. He'd tried to do as Evie asked him, to steel himself to marry Lucy, but he could not. He could not marry a woman he did not love, nevertheless know.

Especially when the woman whom he did love was right at this moment gracing the ballroom he'd just left, her eyes bright with excitement as she talked with her friends, her face as sweet as he remembered it. The time that they had been apart having been torture, and he would no longer be a party to such pain.

He loved her.

Wanted her and damn it all to hell, he'd damn well marry her, no matter what she thought on the issue. No matter that he'd made a mistake in asking Miss Lucy to be his bride. He should never have worried about Lucy's reputation or the scandal to their families should he cry off. She'd run off with another man, for heaven's sake. He was a fool to even think to salvage such a union.

The door to the drawing room opened, and he turned to see Lucy, giggling and clasping the hand of a gentleman he had not seen before. The moment she saw him, her steps faltered, her cheeks turning a bright red that did not suit her at all.

"Your Grace, I did not know you were in here."

He raised one brow, staring down at her and not giving the gentleman a second glance. "So it would seem," he drawled.

Lucy glanced between the man at her side and Finn, working her bottom lip between her teeth. She oozed guilt, and Finn's temper stirred.

"Pray do tell me, Miss Lucy. Who is your acquaintance?"

Lucy's eyes welled with tears, and within a moment of his question, she was seeking a handkerchief from her pocket, her cheeks wet with tears. "I'm so very sorry, Your Grace. This is Mr. Brown and the man that I love. He came back for me, you see."

"Did he now?" Finn drawled, fisting his hand at his side before walking up to the tall, spindly looking fellow. He punched him straight on his nose, sending him careening backward before he landed hard on his ass. Lucy screamed, kneeling beside her fallen rogue, her handkerchief now in use of cleaning up the bastard's bloody nose.

"You broke my nose," the man mumbled, his fingers pinching the bridge of his nose.

"You broke his nose," Lucy gasped, dabbing at the man's face with little effect.

Finn flexed his hand, shrugging. "I do apologize, but I think it was long overdue."

Lucy stood, fisting her hands on her hips. She glowered at him, reminding him of Evie for the first time since he'd met the chit. His stomach clenched, knowing he'd lost Evie and all because of this fickle little troublesome wench before him. He should have thrown being a gentleman aside, allowed her to ruin herself due to her foolish actions, and married Evie as he wished.

Instead, he'd allowed Evie to shoulder her ruination by herself. He did not care that she was of similar age to him, or if she could not give him children. He only wanted her, and if Miss Lucy did not cry off the understanding between them, then he damn well would.

"I cannot marry you, Your Grace. I love Mr. Brown, and he shall be my husband."

Finn chuckled, more than happy with her words. He bowed. "As you wish, Miss Lucy. And let us all hope that this time nothing else calls your Mr. Brown away from you before you marry the rogue. Because this time," he said, leaning close so only she could hear, "I will not be standing to the side to save you, no matter how many tears you shed."

Finn left Lucy gaping after him in the drawing room with her favored Mr. Brown and started for the ballroom, determined to seek out Evie. He needed to find her, to tell her he was sorry and that he was a bastard for not throwing her trouble-making sister to face her ruination, one of her own making, and marry Evie instead.

His actions made him look like a bastard, and he wasn't uncertain that he wasn't one. All he could hope was that Evie would forgive him, allow him to show her that he'd made a mistake, a colossal one, and he was sorry.

~

*E*vie having had enough of the ball and watching her sister fawn over the Duke of Carlisle as if she were in love with him, left the ball and stood in wait while the footman hailed a hackney carriage for her. When one came around the corner, she thanked the servant before giving the coachman her address and stepping inside.

No sooner had she sat on the seat, the carriage lurched to one side, and she watched in both equal parts horror and shock as the Duke of Carlisle joined her, slamming the door closed and tapping the roof to signal they were ready to leave.

She glared at him. "What are you doing here? Have this carriage stopped and get out, Your Grace." He reached for her, and she pushed him away. "Do not touch me, Finn. You have no right to touch me. Not anymore."

"Please, Evie," he pleaded, the sight of his sweet face tempting her more than ever to throw herself into his arms. The thought of Lucy stopped her, and she crossed her arms over her chest to halt her impulsive actions.

"I made a mistake, Evie. A colossal mistake that I hope you'll forgive me for. Give me another chance."

"You're marrying my sister. There is nothing left for us to say."

"There is so much more to say. Please let me try."

Evie stared out the window on Mayfair, watching as the large, opulent homes slipped by. She shouldn't want to give him a chance. He didn't deserve one. Not really. He'd chosen her sister, simply because she cried. Evie sighed, that may not have been the only reason, but even so, she wasn't sure she wanted to allow him to tell her more things that would probably only hurt her.

"Let me explain. I will not leave you alone until you do. I will follow you all about London if I have to."

Evie shook her head at his insistence, but then she supposed she'd never be able to sleep if she did not know what he wanted to say. Never be able to move on with her life, travel abroad, and have her baby if there were things left unsaid between them.

"Very well, what is it that you have to say?"

He gave her a small smile before seemingly steeling himself to speak his truth. "I just spoke with your sister, and our understanding is over. For two reasons. First, before I caught her with Mr. Brown, I had decided to end our betrothal."

"What!" Evie wrenched forward. "What do you mean you just caught Lucy with Mr. Brown? Where? At the ball?" She banged on the roof. "Back to where you picked us up from," she yelled out the window to the driver.

The carriage slowed and turned at the next available corner as Evie turned back to the duke. "You caught Lucy with Mr. Brown? Why ever did you not come and get me? Where is she now? Was she going to run off with him again?"

Finn frowned, holding on to the carriage strap as the vehicle rounded another corner. "I do not know, Evie. She was too busy helping him with his bloody nose."

"Mr. Brown had a bloody nose? Was he injured?"

"Yes," Finn said, clasping her arms and wrenching her to sit beside him on the seat. "Because I bloodied it. First for running away with an innocent woman and then for leaving her alone to find her own way home. I bloodied his nose because he threatened both your and your sister's reputation by acting like a cad. I would bloody anyone's nose who thought to injure you by their actions."

His words trickled into her mind, and Evie forgot about Lucy a moment and more about what he was saying. "You punched him? For me?"

"I did, and I will ensure that this time he does not take flight to Paris before marrying your sister. I will not see your family name tarnished, and yours along with it, due to his behavior."

The carriage rocked to a halt across the street from Lord Hood's home, and Evie heard her sister's voice before she saw her. Lucy was standing on the sidewalk, Mr. Brown beside her, still holding a handkerchief to his nose.

Evie inwardly chuckled at seeing the fiend in such a state. He deserved so much more than a bloodied nose, that was certain. She pushed the window down, leaning out. "Lucy, have Mr. Brown escort you here. I need to speak to you."

Her sister spied her and, pulling Mr. Brown, started across the road, her steps faltering when she spied the Duke of Carlisle inside the carriage. Evie opened the door, without words telling Lucy she needed to get inside.

Lucy sighed but did as she bade, seating her and Mr. Brown across from Evie and the duke. The duke slammed the door closed, wrapping on the roof for the driver to return to her London address. The carriage lurched forward, and so too did Lucy's tirade.

CHAPTER 17

"The duke punched Mr. Brown. Without any warning or need to do so. We deserve an apology."

Evie wondered when her sister became such a little termagant. She'd never been so selfish or self-indulged, but over the past three weeks in London, she had been. Lucy's confidence that the duke would take her back, simply because she bade it, was unlike her. Or at least the girl Evie had known before her flight from Wiltshire with Mr. Brown in any case. Her actions tonight were proof that she never really cared about Finn or anyone but herself.

"His Grace will not be apologizing to anyone, Lucy. I think it is you who needs to apologize and explain what you're about. What is Mr. Brown doing in London? I thought you hightailed it abroad to travel with your friends, sir?" Evie said, staring down her nose at the gentleman. Her attempt at chastising him, reminding him of his error, did little good. Mr. Brown seemed as blind as her sister to the wrong or trouble they had both caused.

TO BE WICKED WITH YOU

"I made a mistake and came back to the woman I love. I only got so far as Devon and turned around."

"How very gentlemanly of you," the duke drawled, watching them all with a disinterested affair.

"Lucy, do you still wish to marry, Mr. Brown? And what of your understanding with the duke?"

"There is no understanding, certainly not after Mr. Brown told me what he learned about His Grace. Not that I care any longer, since the man I do love has returned for me." Her sister crossed her arms, pouting like a child. Evie sighed.

"What did you learn?" the duke asked. Evie felt him stiffen beside her, and she shot a look toward him, noting his hard stare and tense jaw. There could not possibly be any more to this horrendous story that she didn't already know.

"What did you learn, Lucy?" Evie steeled herself, despite not knowing what her sister was about to say. With Finn tense beside her, she couldn't help but think it was severe and not what she wanted to hear.

Lucy smirked, pursing her lips. "Well, as to that, before Mr. Brown left for Devon, he met his traveling companions at Lincon's Inn. He was having lunch and overheard a conversation between Mr. Smithers and one of his work colleagues. You know who Mr. Smithers is, do you not, Your Grace?" Lucy asked, smirking. "They were talking about a time constraint that their client was facing and how it may be solved. That client was the Duke of Carlisle."

"A very interesting conversation." Mr. Brown leaned back on the squabs, a triumphant look crossing his face. "Stating that the Duke of Carlisle required a bride from his home county of Wiltshire and one born from a gentleman or gentry if possible. Mr. Smithers also mentioned that the duke only had sixty days to make it all come to fruition, or he would be facing financial ruin."

"I was that required bride," Lucy put in. "I'm just so very happy that my Mr. Brown came back for me before I married a man who only offered for my hand to keep his thousands of pounds."

"You did not have to say yes, Lucy," Evie stated, wanting to remind her sister that she was just as much to blame for all this mess as the duke was. Not that the news that the duke needed a bride or faced financial ruin was news to her. No, she'd found out that unfortunate information already. She had hoped, however, to save Lucy from that truth.

No woman wanted to hear that any prospective husband only chose her out of necessity. The knowledge that his affections toward her had been due to his fear of losing his fortune left an ache in her chest. They had spent so much time together, had been intimate...that could not have all been false. The duke was capable of love, Evie was sure of it. If the duke was certain of that fact, however, it was another matter entirely.

"You already loved Mr. Brown before the duke offered, you only had to be honest, Lucy."

Lucy gestured toward the duke, who unnervingly remained quiet. "He's the Duke of Carlisle. Who says no to such a man?"

"You should have." Evie digested all this information as the carriage rumbled through Mayfair.

"I must say you're acting very high-handed yourself in all of this, Evie. You knew that I did not want to marry the duke. You agreed to try and dissuade him from me just as I asked."

"You knew that Miss Lucy did not want to be my wife?" The duke stared at her as if he were seeing her for the first time, a stranger he hardly knew instead of a woman who had shared his bed, been a companion. The disappointment in his blue orbs left a hollow feeling inside and she winced. "Why did you not tell me?" he asked.

Evie glared at her sister. How could Lucy involve her in her falsehearted scheme? "I told her to tell you the truth, but before I could make her do so, she'd run off. I agreed to help her, but I was never going to go through with it, I just let her think I would."

"I would not have traveled after your sister had I known that Mr. Brown was indeed who she wanted. I would've let her face the repercussions of her own choice."

"I never asked you to chase after me. I thought that when I ran away, that would've been enough for you to break the understanding."

"Unlike your Mr. Brown, I'm a gentleman," Finn rebuked. "A duke. We do not act in such an ungentlemanly way. We had signed marriage contracts, and unfortunately, I needed a bride and within a short time constraint. You were my only option, and so I had to see if you were sure Mr. Brown was who you wanted before looking elsewhere."

"Well, it certainly seems like you found a replacement with my sister. Have you offered for Evie yet, Your Grace? Or is what Mr. Smithers said about the Milton girls true?"

"What did he say?" Evie demanded, leaning forward. She hated the thought that people were talking about her family, or that others like Mr. Brown could overhear those very conversations.

"That because I was the younger of the Milton sisters, I would suit better since I am of child birthing age. You, a spinster at almost eight and twenty, were past your fertile years. Or so the duke thought."

Evie gasped, her stomach roiling and not only because of her sister's truth but because of the very child she carried that she supposably was too old to bear. How dare the duke be so cruel? So dismissive of a woman who, by the way, was the same age as he.

"No more, Lucy." Evie met her sister's eye and was glad her sibling shut her mouth and lay back, seemingly understanding that she had heard enough. "Your marriage with Mr. Brown will take place next week instead of marrying the duke. A small affair is better, I think, and then you shall retire to Wiltshire and Mr. Brown's farm. Away from Society and any ramifications that you may face due to your actions."

"Why should we hide?" Lucy whined, glaring at the duke. "The duke was more at fault than I was."

"I would have to disagree with that notion." The duke's low, steely tone broke into their conversation, and Evie didn't miss the warning in his words. "I traveled far too many miles these past weeks trying to ensure that your reputation was saved. I did not have to do this. I could have let you throw yourself away, your reputation, and your life. I did not."

"Only because you needed a bride due to financial implications. Not because you cared for my family or me. Your honor and motives are not pure, Your Grace."

"Enough," Evie said, looking between her sister and the duke. The carriage rolled to a halt before her town-house, and she opened the door, stepping out onto the cobbled footpath. Her sister followed, marching into her home. Mr. Brown went to pursue, and Evie stepped in front of the carriage door, stopping him. "You may call on my sister tomorrow afternoon. Good night, Mr. Brown," she said, ignoring her sister's protests before she disappeared inside, grumbling about the unfairness of life and older, interfering siblings.

The duke alighted from the carriage, shutting the door with a decided snap. "I need to speak to you, Miss Milton."

"Tomorrow will do very well for you as well, Your Grace."

The carriage rolled off down the street, and Evie turned, needing to go inside and digest all that she'd learned about the duke, and her sister, whom she decided she did not like very much at the moment. The young woman upstairs did not represent how they had grown up or the morals she thought they both had.

"Please, Evie. Let me come inside."

Evie halted on the step at the duke's plea. Damn her for being weak when it came to him. To want to hear him explain his actions away. She glanced up and down the street, and not seeing anyone and hoping no one was watching from their darkened windows, relented. "Very well, but not for long. I'm fatigued, and in need of solitude after the night we've just endured."

The duke followed her into the house, not saying another word as they reached the front drawing room. Evie closed the door, glad to see that the fire still burned in the room. Molly must have not long retired for the night. She sat before the hearth, clasping her hands in her lap and readying herself to hear the duke out.

He paced before the fire before coming to sit beside her, but still, he said nothing.

Evie had no issue in breaking the silence. "Did you ask for my sister's hand simply to secure your fortune?"

"I did," he said after a moment, shame seeping into his

blue orbs before annoyance replaced that emotion. "And did you agree to try and persuade me to end my betrothal with Lucy? Neither of us is innocent in this."

"I know that," Evie said, hating the fact that she ever agreed to help Lucy. Not that she ever planned to follow through on her scheme, she had planned on making Lucy tell the truth. Not that the duke would believe that. Not now, after the fact. "But I did intend on making Lucy break the engagement that she did not want. She left before I had a chance to make her do so. That is the truth."

The duke rubbed the back of his neck, watching her. "This is madness, Evie. I do not want to quarrel with you."

"Nor I you, but you offered for my sister out of necessity, not because you had any emotional response to her. Was your offer to me the same? How much time do you have left before your father's clause comes into effect?"

"I have only a few weeks before I lose what I need to keep my estates running. I will be left with land and property, but no money."

"So I shall do well enough since my sister is no longer willing or perhaps not, since I'm in my dotage and unable to bear children."

"Forgive me for thinking such a thing. I do not believe that to be true, and I do not see you as a spinster or a woman in her dotage. The assumption was made irresponsibly. My father married in his thirties to a woman ten years his junior. I was only of that opinion because it is what is done, but it is not what I wish to do."

She raised her brow, looking down her nose at him. Not the easiest feat when he sat beside her and even in this position dominated her with his height. "Do you care for me at all, Finn? Or is what I feel for you one-sided?"

"No, of course it is not only on your side." He paused, running a hand through his hair and leaving it on end. "I still require a bride, desperately so, and my father decreed that it must be a woman of good family and from my home county of Wiltshire. I have no doubt the stipulations were so very concise because he wished for me to fail at the quest. He never cared for his son, probably why he stopped coming to my mother's bed once I had been born. He cared only for himself and his whores. He was an infamous rogue that London loved to hate."

The duke reached out and picked up her hands, holding them firm. "What I feel for you, Evie, is nothing like what I felt for your sister. While I liked her, it is you that I long to see, to hear, and spend time with. It's you that captured my heart."

She wanted to believe him. The time that they had spent together, she had lost her heart to the duke. In fact, she feared on their first night at the Bear Inn, where he'd held her close during the night, allowing her to keep warm was when she'd first suspected her heart had been touched.

Even so, it did not change the fact that he'd chased down her sister simply to marry her to satisfy some will. Of course, a duke needed funds to run his estates, but to make a woman believe she was desired, wanted when not, was not the act of a gentleman. How could she trust him to be telling the truth now? That she was different. That she was desired and loved.

"You lied to me. To my family."

"I was not alone in my untruth," he shot back, silencing her. "Did you and your sister plan how to end the understanding? Did you think to seduce me? Were your actions in my bed all feigned?"

Evie gasped. How dare he ask her that. "I would never

do such a thing, and if you knew me at all, you would know that for the lie it is."

"Evie," he sighed, squeezing her hands a little. "Why did you not tell me that Lucy was in love with someone else? All the time we were together I felt as if I were being torn in two. Between honor and what I desire, what I want. I repeatedly chastised myself for the choice I made, for it was the wrong one. If I knew that my concern was not warranted, that I could act on my desires, my wishes, without feeling like I was replicating my father, a scoundrel who enjoyed scandal and acting without honor, our time together could have been so much better."

"You were set on bringing her home. Your reminding my father of the money you paid him along with the marriage contracts was always in the back of my mind. How could I tell you? I figured that once you did see Lucy, married and happy, that it wouldn't matter what she asked me to do for her actions made her plan moot in the end."

"I have long forgiven that debt. I will not be making your father repay me if that is your concern."

"I did not think you would," Evie admitted, wanting to tell him that there was more to say between them. That she was carrying his child, but she wanted him to choose her for herself, not because he needed a wife. "What do we do now?" she asked, hating the trepidation in her tone. For all that had occurred, she did not want to lose the duke, but nor would she marry him simply to ensure his riches.

"What indeed," the duke drawled, meeting her gaze.

∼

*F*inn wanted to pull Evie into his arms and kiss away her fear, her doubts. He needed her to know that he adored her and only her and bedamned his father's will and clause overshadowing his life, turning it upside down.

"Evie," he said, kneeling before her. "Know that what I'm about to ask you is done so because to my very core, it is what I want. Know that what I'm about to ask you is asked because I love you, more than any inheritance, or honor a man can have. I ask you this because I want you and no one else, and had I realized that sooner I could have saved everyone a lot of trouble and strife."

She shifted on her chair. Her beautiful dark eyes focused on his every word. "What did you wish to ask me?"

So many things, more than he could count. "My first question would be, Evie, from this day forward, will you do me the extreme honor of becoming my wife? Marry me and be my duchess just as you should always have been."

His heart beat fast in his chest, beating a crescendo that he was sure she could hear. The clock on the mantle clicked the seconds away, and still, she did not speak. The fire crackled in the grate, and he fought for patience, needing to know what she was thinking. "Evie? Will you marry me?"

She threw him a small smile, and a little part of him rejoiced. Hopeful that she would give him a second chance. Everyone deserved one, surely. "Are you certain that I'm not too old to be your bride? What if I'm unable to have children?"

"I do not care, so long as I have you. You mean more to me than anything I do not have, already have, or may never have. Did you hear what I said, my love?" he asked

167

when she remained quiet. "I love you. I want you. From this day forward and forever. Tell me you feel the same and pull me from this torture that I have been living with these past three weeks."

She smiled, her eyes warming upon him. "I'm so glad that you said what you just did, for I too feel the same way."

Finn leaned forward on his knees, coming eye level with her. "Marry me. Marry me as soon as I can gain a special license. I do not want to spend another night away from you."

She slipped her arms over his shoulders, and heat licked down his spine. He'd missed her. So very much that at times he thought he would go mad with want of her. A life with Evie would forever be an adventure, just as their travels had, and he could not wait to start the journey.

"I will marry you," she said, at last, closing the space between them and kissing him gently on the lips. The embrace was short and chaste and nowhere near what he needed, wanted from his future bride. "I love you too," she admitted.

Finn pulled her into his arms, never wanting to let her go. He took her mouth in a searing kiss, one that had been building for the past weeks back in town. Her tongue melded with his, and his body shot to life for the first time since she walked out of his life.

"I want you," he said, kissing his way across her cheek to nibble on her ear. She had the prettiest ears he'd ever seen, and tonight with the little diamond pendant hanging from them, they made her look even more beautiful if that were possible. "Under me and in your bed tonight. I do not want to leave," he whispered into her ear, feeling a slight shiver rake through her body.

"I want that too." She gasped as his hand cupped one breast, his thumb and finger finding her nipple and rolling it between the two pads. "This is wicked, you understand. Are you certain you do not want to wait until we're married?"

"I could not keep my hands from you these past weeks. I'm not about to start doing so now. You will be my wife in a day or so. I see no harm in us coming together."

"Hmm," she said, standing and pulling him up to stand before her. He towered over her, and he could not help but run his hands over the soft, delectable flesh of her face. Hell, she was beautiful, sweet, and his.

All his.

He scooped her up into his arms, ignoring her protests that they would be seen and strode from the room. "Where is your bedroom?" he asked when they made the top of the stairs, Evie turning a deep shade of red when they passed a startled footman.

"Second door on your left," she said, playing with the hair on his nape.

Her touch drove him insane, and he breathed deep, calming himself. They would be alone soon, and then they could take all the time they wanted. And before this week ended, she would be the new Duchess of Carlisle. Just as she always should have been.

Her bedroom door was ajar, and he pushed it open, kicking it shut with his foot. Relief poured through him that he was hers, and she was his, and soon no one and nothing could rip her from him again. Not family, scandal, or steadfast honor.

Nothing.

CHAPTER 18

*E*vie stood beside the Duke of Carlisle in the beautiful St George's Parish church in Hanover square and exchanged vows with His Grace. As promised, he'd secured a special license, and two days after asking for her hand, she was marrying him. Her friends stood in the pews behind them, each of them unable to hide their pleasure, just as Evie was unable to stop the smile on her lips.

The duke turned and repeated the vows the priest spoke, and warmth flowed through her veins. He stood beside her, dressed in a superfine coat of dark blue. His cravat highlighted his sweet face, and it took all of her concentration not to throw herself into his arms, just as they had been doing the past two days. He'd insisted she traveled with him to Doctor's Commons in London to get the special license from the Archbishop of Canterbury. Being back in the carriage with His Grace alone for some time ended up being quite an enjoyable ride.

The priest announced them husband and wife, and he took her arm, turning to smile at their friends.

Married at last.

*L*ater that morning, they stood in the gardens of the duke's London home, celebrating their wedding ceremony. Tomorrow they were returning to Wiltshire to inform her parents of their marriage and to see her sister wed. Lucy had returned home the previous day, having stated that she wanted to marry Mr. Brown in their family church in Marlborough. Her mother and father had traveled with Lucy and her betrothed, wanting to ensure that Lucy did, in fact, return home to be married.

Evie had not told her parents of the duke's offer. They would find out soon enough, and she did not need them at her wedding. When she returned home, there would be time for a celebration.

"What a handsome husband you have," Molly said, passing Evie a glass of champagne and smiling over to the duke, who spoke with Whitstone, Lord Duncannon, and Marquess Ryley.

"Isn't he?" Evie agreed, hoping their wedding breakfast would be over soon so she could be alone with him. She had not told him of the child, but she would today. He'd married her without knowing that she was pregnant. She didn't want to state her vows with any doubt that he was making her his wife because he loved her, not because she was carrying his child. "I'm so happy, Molly, and sad too. We will no longer be living together."

Molly waved her concerns away, sipping her drink. "Never mind that. You know that I'm more than happy to visit my family in Hertfordshire. Then, as planned, I shall be traveling abroad to France. I wish to see Paris again, and then when I am home, perhaps you shall allow me to follow you all about during the London seasons, so I shall have something to occupy my time. I may be unmarried and have two or three strands of gray hair on my head, but there is still plenty of fun to be had, and I'm determined to have it."

"And you shall," Evie agreed, linking arms with her oldest friend. "You are more than welcome to stay with us during the Season or whenever you wish. My door is always open to you. I cannot thank you enough for being my companion and support these past weeks. I know I have not been the sanest person at times."

"You thought that you had lost the love of your life. That is enough to make anyone a little mad."

"Who is mad?" the duke asked, wrapping his arm about Evie's waist and holding her close to his side.

"I was, husband, when I thought that I had lost you."

He leaned down, kissing her promptly in front of their friends. The kiss, a sweet embrace, lingered longer than it ought and a few muffled chuckles from about them brought them to their senses. "You will never lose me, my darling. I promise you that," the duke whispered so only she could hear.

Ava, Hallie, and Willow joined them. All of her friends here made the day more special, and she was thankful for their love and support.

"Well," Willow said, a teasing glint in her eye. "Now, there was only one."

"One what?" Molly asked, looking at them all in turn.

"One of us left unwed. Whatever shall we do, ladies? I suggest that next Season we promise to all be in town to ensure our darling Molly finds the gentleman of her dreams," Ava said, grinning mischievously.

"I beg you not to do such a thing," Molly said, shaking

her head. "I'm traveling abroad, as you well know. I may not even be back before next year."

"You will be, we'll make sure of it. There are some acquaintances of Whitstone's that I know are suitable and honorable for our Molly. I shall hold a ball and invite them."

"Please do not." Molly shook her head, her face paling somewhat. "I will not be bargained off like a prized mare of yours, Ava."

Evie smiled at her friends as they planned and schemed for Molly. Finn took her hand and pulled her away toward the house, her friends so caught up in their conversation they did not notice their parting.

"What are you up to, Finn?"

"I think our friends have had us for long enough. It's time for you and me to become better acquainted as husband and wife."

She raised her brow, unable to keep a smile from her lips. "Really? How very naughty of you."

"You have no idea." Finn pulled her through his town-house without, thankfully, passing a servant. To see them, it would not be hard to know what they were about. Evie chuckled at the thought just as he pulled her into the ducal apartments in the home, closing and locking the door with a decided snap.

He leaned against the painted wooden door, slowly dragging the cravat from his neck before throwing it aside. The top button on his breeches was next, and heat licked across her skin, expectation thrumming through her core.

"You are impatient."

"I am." He pushed away from the door and came up against her within a couple of strides. He hoisted her in his arms, kissing her soundly as he made his way to the bed.

Evie expected him to throw her onto the opulent bedding, but he did not. Instead, he set her on her feet, turning her, so she faced the bed. "Put your hands down to support yourself."

She did as he bade, expectation flowing through her. She could feel herself grow wet, and she wiggled her bottom against Finn, wanting him with a desperation that left her breathless.

Cool air kissed her legs as his large hands clasped the hem of her gown, sliding it up to her waist. Evie bit her lip, thinking how delightful married life was already.

Naughty indeed.

~

*F*inn's cock had been in a state of semi-erection since he'd seen his beautiful Evie walking up toward him to become his wife. He'd chatted and entertained their friends in the gardens for as long as he could, but all he could think about was when he'd have his bride to himself.

Alone in his bed. His duchess next to him in the ducal apartments.

The duchess, of course, had her own suite of rooms both here and at their numerous country estates, but he wanted Evie to sleep with him. To only ever be within an arms reach of his side.

His wife mewled as he glided his hand up her thigh, slipping it against her mons and teasing her wet cunny. She was hot and ready for him, and with his other hand, he freed his cock, taking himself in hand.

"I'm going to fuck you, Duchess," he said, lifting the

last of her gown and thrusting his cock against her sex, teasing her with slow, delicious strokes.

"Oh yes," she gasped, her hands fisting into the bedding. She slid back onto him, teasing him in turn. "Fuck me, Finn."

Her taunting words maddened him, and without waiting, he thrust deep into her. His hands anchored on her hips, holding her as she took each thrust. She was so tight, grinding down on him, and he breathed deep, wanting to pleasure her as much as she did him. He could not get enough of her.

Finn pushed Evie onto the bed. "Get on your hands and knees, my darling."

She scrambled to do as he asked, and he came over her. He slipped into her again, and exquisite pleasure made them both moan. From the first time they had been together, each time was the same. The enjoyment they wrought was something he would never tire of. Finn thrust his cock, finding a fast, delectable rhythm Evie liked. She panted and moaned before him, dropping to muffle her noises in the bedding.

He pushed her toward a climax, teasing himself in turn. Her cunny wrapped about him like a glove, milking him and his breathing seized. She was so beautiful, so willing and his.

The word *mine* reverberated about in his mind, and he held himself deep in her, smiling as she undulated against him, seeking him, wanting him to fuck her.

"What are you doing? Stop teasing me, Finn."

Finn came down over her, one hand slipping down her bodice to clasp her breast, tease her puckered, erect nipples. They fit into his palms and he was impatient to kiss them, lick his way down her delectable body to between her legs and take her to climax with his tongue.

So many things to do and now they had all the time in the world to do it in.

Not willing to wait any longer, she pushed back onto him, fucking him instead. His body seized, and he groaned, pumping her anew. Their lovemaking became frenzied the closer they came to pleasure.

Finn moaned as the trembling contractions of her release pulled and tightened about his cock, and he came, hard and long, fucking her until she collapsed on the bed, still dressed in her wedding gown, but satisfied beyond reason.

He slumped beside her, chuckling at their dressed state and what they had done. "At least this way, we can return to the wedding breakfast, and no one will be any the wiser."

"Really?" Evie said, sitting up and pulling the pins from her hair.

"What are you doing?" he asked, unable to form enough energy to stop her progress.

"We're not going back to the breakfast, husband. You're going to make love to me all day and all night. If you did not already know, I'm seven and twenty. I have some years to make up for being without a husband."

He grinned, pulling at his cravat. "Well, I cannot say no to that."

She came down over him, kissing him before moving down his neck. "No, you cannot. And now that I have you right where I want you, there is something else that I'd like to try."

"Hmm? What is that?" he said, closing his eyes and enjoying her touch.

"Well, what I want to kiss next is in your breeches, so please, Your Grace, do lie back, and let me explore what is now mine."

Finn groaned, his cock twitching at the thought of seeing Evie take him in her mouth. The idea alone could almost make him come. He lay his arms behind his head, grinning. "I'm all yours, Duchess."

"Yes, you most certainly are," Her Grace agreed.

~

*E*vie woke the next morning, her stomach cramping and protesting the new day. She pushed back the blankets and flew out of bed, running toward the chamber pot behind the screen and retched. Only just making it in time. Her stomach roiled as it always did during this time of the morning and she slumped back against the wall, hoping that the nausea would pass sooner rather than later.

However, she would deal with such an unwelcome side effect to a most precious gift.

"Evie? Are you poorly?" Finn came around the screen and kneeled before her, reaching out to touch her forehead. "You are a little warm and clammy. Was it something you ate?"

He helped her to stand and then swooped her into his arms, walking them both back toward the bed. Evie basked against his warm, calming presence, before he laid her down on the bedding, tucking her back in. The perfect husband, he poured her a glass of water, handing it to her. "Do you wish for me to ring for a tisane? A bath? What will make you feel better, my darling?"

Evie reached out, pulling him to sit beside her.

"Nothing will make me feel better for a little while at least. You must prepare yourself to be putting up with such annoyances for some weeks still. Or so my doctor advised me when I met with him the other week."

The duke frowned down at her, his face a mask of confusion. "Whatever is wrong? There must be something we can do. You cannot be ill like that every morning, surely."

Evie chuckled, sipping her water. "The sickness the doctor advised will pass, Finn. He says by the fourth month I shall be quite myself again." She was being vague, wanting him to guess their happy news, which if his widened eyes and gaping mouth were anything to go by, he'd figured out her secret.

"You're pregnant?"

She nodded, tears welling in her eyes at the welcome news. A baby. Their baby. "I am. I know I should have told you earlier, but I was fearful. Silly really," she said, wiping at her cheeks. "I should have trusted in your love."

"You thought that had you told me I would have only married you out of obligation, out of necessity due to my father's ridiculous will." Finn joined her in bed, pulling her up against his chest. "I'm glad you did not tell me. Now not you nor anyone else can ever think that I married you out of such reasons. I married you because I love you." He kissed her soundly, taking her cup of water and placing it on the table beside their bed. "I adore you. I cannot tell you how happy this news makes me."

"Truly?" she asked, clasping him tight. "I'm so glad. I was a little worried you would think it was too soon."

"No," he said, meeting her gaze, the love that shone in his blue orbs making her heart squeeze. "A child with you, to start our family, would never be too soon."

Evie reached up and touched his jaw, feeling the short stubble against her palms. He was so very handsome and dishevelled after their night of lovemaking and sleep. How she adored him. "I'm so glad you said that, my love for I couldn't agree more."

"We should travel back to Wiltshire. You need to rest and my housekeeper at Stoneheim will know exactly how to make you comfortable, so you do not suffer unduly."

The idea of returning home was appealing. The country air, her mama to help her through the coming months. "I would like that very much."

"Wonderful." Finn jumped out of bed, racing to ring for the servants. "We'll leave today if you agree."

"I most definitely agree," Evie said, before another cramping pain took hold in her stomach and she raced out of bed for the second time that morning.

The duke came about the screen, rubbing her back. "On second thought, maybe when your sickness calms down, we shall return home. There is no rush."

Evie nodded, heaving once again into the chamber pot. "I think that may be best."

EPILOGUE

The Season, London – One year later

*E*vie rocked the cribs of Marcus Finlay Stone, Marquess of Lexington, and Lady Marigold Stone in their newly decorated London bedroom. She had just read them a bedtime story, and tonight she and Finn were going to attend their first ball of the Season since their marriage. Evie bent down, giving her wolfhound, Sugar a big pat and scratch before taking her leave.

They had not returned to town after they had traveled back to Wiltshire, preferring to stay in the country for the duration of her confinement and because the duke had long lost interest in the *ton*.

But, duty called, and she had promised her friends that she would attend next year's Season if only to ensure their friend Molly found a husband as wonderful and sweet as they all had.

"Are you ready, my dear?" Finn said, stepping into the room, his skintight black breeches and superfine coat with a silver embroidered waistcoat made him look beyond handsome. Nerves fluttered in her stomach, and she had the urge to pinch herself that he was hers—all hers and no one else's.

"I'm just putting our babies to bed. Are they not adorable?"

Finn smiled, coming into the room and kissing each of their children in turn. He pulled her from the room, wishing the nanny a goodnight and telling her where they could be found if they needed to return home.

"I know you're nervous about leaving them, but all will be well. They're safe and happy and about to go to sleep. Nanny will look after them and I need to look after you. You deserve a little fun and to see your friends again. It's almost been a year."

"I know," Evie said, walking down the stairs and taking a shawl from a waiting footman. Finn helped her into the carriage, and he rapped on the roof. The carriage rolled forward, and Evie glanced back at the house, praying all would be well.

"You're a wonderful mother. I'm so very happy that you're mine."

Warmth spread through her, and she turned toward Finn, snuggling up against him as they so often did when traveling alone. "And you're a good father. Thank you for the wonderful, full life that you've given me."

Tears pooled in her eyes and she sniffed, knowing that not all her emotion was due to her love of Finn, but also being away from her precious babies for the first time. She took a calming breath, repeating what Finn had told her. That all would be well. The children were well looked after.

"Are you really going to try and match Molly with a gentleman that you ladies believe is suitable? I could not help but feel she is less than enthused to be a party to your plan if her words the other afternoon at tea were anything to go by."

Evie shot a look at the duke. "Really? I thought she seemed quite open to our helping her."

Finn scoffed, smiling. "You are all blind if you think that is the case. Molly looked like she could spit fire, not to mention I have heard rumors."

"Rumors? What kind of rumors?" Oh dear, Evie hoped there was nothing wrong with her friend. She had not spoken much about her trip abroad, only that it was pleasant and something that she would love to do again.

"Rumors that she was somehow involved with a certain duke in Italy. He's English, has lived abroad for many years, indeed, has houses in both Italy, Spain, and England. A rogue, of course, never married and unlikely to do so, but he's in London for the Season, and it's quite the scandal."

"He's here? Whatever brought him back to England, do you think?"

Finn grinned down at her, winking. "What brought him back to England indeed? Can you not guess, my dear?"

Evie stared at her husband a moment, hardly able to believe it. "Molly?"

The duke kissed her, smiling. "Yes. Molly."

Dear Reader,

Thank you for taking the time to read *To Be Wicked with You*! I hope you enjoyed the fourth book in my League of Unweddable Gentlemen series. I do adore a good carriage ride adventure, and if you wanted to see where Evie and Finn stayed, I have all the details on my Pinterest page. Follow this link here to see those lovely historical inns.

I adore my readers, and I'm so thankful for your support with my books. If you're able, I would appreciate an honest review of *To Be Wicked with You*. As they say, feed an author, leave a review!

If you'd like to learn about the fifth book in my League of Unweddable Gentlemen series, *Kiss Me, Duke*, please read on. I have included chapter one for your reading pleasure.

Tamara Gill

KISS ME, DUKE

LEAGUE OF UNWEDDABLE GENTLEMEN, BOOK 5

Molly Clare is living her dream. Being a guest in a gorgeous villa while she explores Rome is everything she could've hoped for and more. The man who owns the villa is equally charming—and entirely too tempting. At least, that's what he appears to be. The truth of who and what he really is…well, that's infinitely more complicated.

· · ·

Lord Hugh Farley is living a nightmare. Ruined by rumors of indiscretions he didn't commit and betrayed by his own family, his only option was to leave London. But any hope he had for a quiet Roman exile is destroyed when she arrives. Molly is everything he's ever wanted...and nothing he can have. But keeping his mind—and hands—off her quickly proves impossible.

Can Molly and Hugh find a way to clear his name and build a future together? Or is their happily ever after nothing but a fantasy?

CHAPTER 1

Rome Italy, 1829

They had arrived. Finally. Molly stepped out of the carriage and stretched, basked in the warm Mediterranean sun that warmed her blood and healed the many aches and pains from weeks of travel. Rome. Just the thought of where she was sent a thrill down her spine and expectation thrumming through her blood.

So many wonderful places to visit and see, and thanks to her wonderful friends back in London, and the Duke of Whitstone, month-long lodgings at the Villa Maius had been secured for her. The gentleman who resided here was from home, but his servants would care for her and her companion for the short time they would be in the city.

The front door to the villa opened, and a gray-haired, voluptuous woman came out onto the street, her smile as warm as the sun shining down on her back.

"*Signora*, Molly Clare, welcome. Welcome to Rome. Come, we shall serve refreshments for you. You must be exhausted."

Molly smiled, relieved to be welcomed so lovingly at the home. She did not know anything of Mr. Farley, who lived here, other than he was friends with the Duke of Whitstone. There had always been a little niggling concern within her that the staff may be annoyed at her arrival, being unknown to them as she was, but it would not seem to be so.

"Thank you for having me. I hope it is not too much trouble that I'm here." She walked in off the street into a small foyer that led onto a large, rectangular room partly roofed. A fountain sat in its center, a naked cherub squirting water from his mouth. Looking up, Molly noted the opening in the roof sat directly over the fountain, and in ancient times, it would be the place the villa would have collected its water for the family.

"Oh, no no no. We're very happy to have you here." The servant ordered a tall, dark-haired man to attend to the luggage while she walked them toward a set of stairs. "Mr. Armstrong is not here. He is away in Naples for the duration of your stay, and we have been expecting you. He informed us all before he left last month to care for you well. You have mutual friends, yes?"

Molly looked about the villa. Mosaic-tiled floors adorned the space, images of Roman life, of agricultural scenes and animals. All lower-floor rooms had their windows open, the curtains billowing with the warm, Mediterranean air. The breeze smelled of salt and spices, of oranges and freshly cut grass. She stopped a moment, taking in the view from one of the windows she could see through a doorway. The courtyard garden, full of olive trees, beckoned her to sit and savor its beauty.

"We do, yes. The Duke of Whitstone. Although I have

never met Mr. Armstrong, I am very grateful to him for allowing me to stay here."

The housekeeper beamed, seemingly well pleased at her compliment of her employer. "He is the best of men whom I'm sorry you shall not have the honor of meeting." The woman started up the stone stairs. "I'm Maria, my dear, the housekeeper of Villa Maius. Should you need anything at all, merely let me know, and I shall do all that I can to make your stay enjoyable."

"Thank you." They climbed the stairs, the second floor opened up to a large, rectangular room with reclining wicker chairs. A balcony stood at the end of the room. Molly could not pass without taking in the view. She stepped out onto the balcony, the breath catching in her lungs. The view overlooked the street they had entered on. At this height, it gave her a better vantage point of the city beyond. Rome. Its glory spread out before her like a gift from the gods. Her fingers curled around the stone balustrade, anchoring herself so she would not run from the villa and see firsthand the ancient city. Sounds wafted up to tease her and urge her to leave and explore.

Soon, she promised. As soon as she had bathed and had a restoring cup of tea.

"The center of Rome is only a short walk from here. At the other end of the villa is another room similar to this that overlooks the river Tiber. I can always have the carriage put at your disposal, however, if you do not want to walk. To see the Vatican, you shall have to avail yourself of the vehicle."

Excitement thrummed through her veins, and she leaned out over the railing, spying a few people out on the streets, some taking in the sights while others plied their trade. "What a magnificent city. I have always wanted to tour, and now I can. I cannot believe it."

"I am dreading the return journey, however," her companion, Miss Sinclair said, joining her and staring down at the city with a disgruntled air. "Shall we have tea?"

Molly was reluctant to leave the magnificent view, one she longed to be part of, and nor would she allow Miss Sinclair's dislike of the distances they had traversed to dampen her excitement. If her companion did not wish to see Rome, she could stay here at the villa. Molly went about London most of the time on her own, it would not be out of character for her.

"Yes, let's, and then I can get started on exploring this wonderful city."

"Would you like to have tea on the balcony, *Signora* Molly?"

"Thank you, yes," she replied, seeing the outdoor setting and sitting. Servants bustled about the home, bringing up their trunks to the rooms. Molly could almost pinch herself just to confirm that she was indeed here in Rome. Her time was precious, only a month, and then they would be on the return journey back to England. Travel would take several weeks, and she wanted to visit some other cities on the continent before returning to London and the new Season.

The tea was sweet and refreshing, and lovingly the housekeeper had made some biscuits with almonds through them, which squelched her rumbling stomach.

Molly leaned back in her chair, placing down her napkin, well-sated after the fleeting repast. "Shall we finish the tour of the house, see our rooms and then decide where to go first?"

"Of course, Miss Molly," Miss Sinclair said, yawning.

It had been a long day, but Molly was too excited, had waited too long to be in Rome to lie down for the afternoon. She wanted to explore, walk the streets, visit the markets, and be part of the culture here in this ancient city.

"If you're tired, Miss Sinclair, I can always go out without you. I do not mind."

Miss Sinclair's lips pursed into a disapproving, thin line. "No, that would never do. You need to have a chaperone and company to keep you safe. I will simply have to endure it."

"I do not wish for you to endure Rome. I want you to enjoy it as much as I intend on doing."

"I do not believe that will be possible, Miss Molly. I have an aversion to heat, and if it did not escape your notice, it is very hot outside."

Molly turned toward the balcony, the slight breeze wafting in through the doors cooled her skin. Yes it was warm, but England was always so very cold. How could anyone not make use of such beautiful weather and explore it?

The housekeeper stepped forward, catching Molly's eye. "We have a manservant here, Miss Clare. He would be more than happy to escort you about Rome so you may see some of our wonderful city."

Molly smiled at Miss Sinclair. "See, I shall be perfectly safe. You may have this afternoon to rest and recuperate, and we shall come together for dinner this evening before tonight's ball."

"You intend to attend Lord and Lady Dalton's ball this evening? Even though we only arrived today?"

"Of course I intend to go." Molly shook her head at

her companion, having gained the sense that she did not want to go or do anything while they were here. The prospect was not helpful, nor would it be possible. Molly had four weeks to visit this wonderful city, and she would simply have to ignore her companion's complaints about seeing everything they could in that time.

"Maria, will you show me to my room, please?"

The housekeeper bustled down a wide passageway until she came to a room that overlooked more of the villa grounds, lawns, and gardens that swam with a variety of colors. The tinkling sound of water carried up to her, and she looked for the fountain but could not see it from her room. She would have to go downstairs to find it herself.

Her room was a tiled mosaic floor that was made out in a variety of blossoming flowers. Her bed was large, opulent with its coverlet and abundance of pillows. She, too, was partial to lots of pillows on beds. It somehow made them look complete. Perfect.

A small writing desk occupied the space before one window, and a large settee sat before her fire. Although she did not believe she would need that at all while she was here in Rome. Not with it being so warm.

"There is freshwater and linens behind the screen for you, Miss Molly. When you're ready to go out, come downstairs, and I shall fetch Marcus for you. He will keep you safe and show you all the best sites Rome has on offer."

"Thank you so much. I cannot tell you how thrilled I am about being here."

The housekeeper smiled before leaving her to her ablutions, the sound of Miss Sinclair's voice as she was taken to her room echoing down the hall.

Molly walked to the small balcony her room had and

glanced down at the garden. She raised her face to the sun, breathing deep. What an idyllic location to live. One could get used to such a place and never return home to rainy, dreary old London.

Want to read more? Purchase, Kiss Me, Duke today!

LORDS OF LONDON SERIES
AVAILABLE NOW!

Dive into these charming historical romances! In this six-book series, Darcy seduces a virginal duke, Cecilia's world collides with a roguish marquess, Katherine strikes a deal with an unlucky earl and Lizzy sets out to conquer a very wicked Viscount. These stories plus more adventures in the Lords of London series! Available now through Amazon or read free with KindleUnlimited.

Lords of London

KISS THE WALLFLOWER SERIES
AVAILABLE NOW!

If the roguish Lords of London are not for you and wall-flowers are more your cup of tea, this is the series for you. My Kiss the Wallflower series, are linked through friendship and family in this four-book series. You can grab a copy on Amazon or read free through KindleUnlimited.